Woodsmoke

Eileen D Frost

Published in 2008 by YouWriteOn.com

First Edition

Published by YouWriteOn.com

Foreword to Woodsmoke

Many of the events in the story really took place, although I have changed the names of the characters to avoid any misunderstandings. I have had to rely on memory and the internet for dates of some of the events, and I apologise for any errors spotted by keen-eyed readers who happened to live in Portsmouth or Horndean at the time.

Eileen D Frost

Dedication

Woodsmoke is dedicated to all those children who lived through the Second World War and experienced the horrors of nights spent underground sheltering from air raids, the loss of friends and relatives, evacuation, shortages, interrupted schooling (although that was more of a bonus than a horror), and never knowing whether the next bomb would have their name on it. Now in their seventies or eighties, this story, although written mainly for children, will I hope bring back memories of the never-to-be-forgotten era of the Second World War.

Chapter One

April 1943

'Air raids don't scare me,' said Billy Parkin to his friend Dave Spiller as they left school one Friday afternoon, and the wail of the siren spread across the city of Portsmouth. 'I like to hear the whistle of bombs as they pass overhead. My dad says that if you can hear the whistle, it's goin' to drop on someone else, an' not you. *He* says that if a bomb has your name on it, it will get you wherever you are.'

'I don't believe that,' Dave said.

'Besides,' Billy went on, 'you are just as likely to get blown to bits in an air raid shelter as outside. That's what my dad says anyway.'

'Your dad knows a lot of things.'

'Yeah, he does.'

'D'you want to come in my shelter?' Dave, who lived across the road from the school, offered.

'No, I'll be all right,' Billy said. 'See you tomorrow morning. Roy Rogers is on at the Regal.' They parted company and, keeping one ear cocked for the sound of German aeroplanes, Billy sauntered past the shops, grey cap askew on his dark hair, socks in a concertina around his ankles. He had farther to go than Dave but it didn't bother him.

He turned at the sound of running footsteps, to see his younger sister Jess, red in the face and dark brown pigtails bouncing, catching him up. 'Hurry up,' she called out as she raced past without slowing down. 'We've got to get home.' When she reached the corner of Chessell road, where they lived, she stopped, and Billy saw her clutch at her side.

'What's the matter with you?' he said as he caught up with her.

'Stitch,' she panted, her face screwed up with pain

'Serves you right. You shouldn't have been runnin'. There's nothin' to be scared of.' She took a swing at him with her satchel. 'There's an air raid on, in case you didn't know,' she said.

A Corporation dustcart sat in the middle of Chessell Road, and despite the air raid warning, the dustmen carried on emptying the contents of bins into the side of the cart. The drone of a German aeroplane caught Billy's attention and he looked up. It seemed to be hovering just above the clouds, waiting. Then everything happened so quickly that he had no time to think. The clouds parted, the aeroplane nosedived through the gap and the rat-tat-tat-tat of machine-gun fire echoed down the road. A hail of bullets ricocheted along the pavement where only seconds before, he and Jess had been walking. Dustbins flew in every direction, hitting the pavement in a clatter of metal on stone as the men dived for shelter. Jess let out a scream, someone bawled at them to take cover and Billy grabbed hold of her. 'Under here. Quick!' he shouted, pushing her to the ground.

They flattened themselves under a privet hedge, and Billy ordered her to keep still. The aircraft rose and circled, dived again and he could almost smell the heat of bullets as another round skittered along the pavement just inches away from where they lay. Even during the worst of the blitz, he hadn't felt this scared. His shirt, now soaked in sweat, clung to him and he could hear his heart beating so fast, it sounded like a drum in his ears. He hadn't said his prayers for a long time, but now, he said aloud, 'Please, Jesus don't let us get killed.'

He heard a yelp and raised his head. A dog, its body twisted, lay in the gutter in a pool of its own blood. Although he had seen some awful things on the Pathe News at the Regal, the sight of an innocent little dog riddled with bullets made him feel sick. He stuffed his fist into his mouth, propped himself up on one elbow and watched as one of the dustmen scrambled to his feet and ran to the aid of the animal. It looked dead, its eyes fixed in a terrified stare at the sky. When the man picked the animal up and, unable to find a collar, tossed it into the dustcart, Billy had to look away.

Presently, the roar of the enemy aircraft grew fainter as it turned and flew out to sea. As the all clear sounded, Billy helped Jess to her feet. 'Don't you dare tell our mum about this,' he said as they ran the rest of the way home, reaching the Anderson shelter in their front garden as the wail of the siren died away. 'An' stop snivellin'.' He lifted the door out of its slot and stared into the astonished face of their mother, Doris.

'What on earth d'you think you're doing?' she yelled at them. 'Have you taken leave of your senses? How many times do I have to tell you to find a public shelter if you're caught out in a raid?'

Billy pulled a face and shot a warning look at Jess. If their mother found out about the machine-gunning, she'd go mad. 'We were all right, Mum,' he said. 'When the siren went off, we lay under old man Potter's hedge until it was over. Didn't we, Jess?' He looked at his sister and she looked at her feet.

'Oh, did you now? And where were you when all those bullets hit the pavement?'

'Under the hedge, like I said.' Billy hadn't realised his mother would have heard all the noise in the street.

'Well, in future, just do as you're told and take shelter. The pair of you could have been killed.'

'*Yes*, Mum,' they said, together.

The following morning at ten o'clock, Billy met Dave at the Regal. The two boys, friends since infant's school, stood in the queue.

'Got any sweets?' Dave asked.

Billy shook his head. 'I used all my coupons up on Monday,' he said. 'Taskers sweet shop had some chocolate in.'

Dave reached into his jacket pocket and pulled out a bag of mint humbugs. 'Here,' he said, 'you can have these.'

'What about you?'

'I've still got some coupons left over from last week.'

'Thanks, Dave. I'll let you have some of mine next Saturday.'

Dave laughed. 'Yeah, I bet,' he said.

They watched Roy Rogers in "The Man from Cheyenne", the Pathe News, and a Disney cartoon. On the way home, Billy told Dave about the machine-gunning. 'I thought we were goin' to die,' he said. 'And, *boy* was my mum mad.'

'You should've come in my shelter.'

'Yeah, I know.'

'Anyway,' Dave said, 'I might see you in the park tomorrow, if I'm allowed. If not, I'll see you at school on Monday. An' don't be late.'

'I won't.' Billy watched his friend walk away towards his own home. The two boys were close friends and would do anything for each other. They looked almost like brothers, with the same dark hair and brown eyes, except that Dave stood a foot taller than Billy and had started to fill out. Billy, according to his mother, still looked like a nine-penny rabbit, despite his enormous appetite. As he strolled home, Billy made up his mind that he'd hang onto his sweet ration next week. Instead of spending it all at once on Monday as he usually did, he'd save it to share with Dave next Saturday.

The siren woke everyone up in the middle of that night and Billy, his eyes heavy from sleep, scrambled out of bed and pulled a jumper over his pyjamas. He met his mother on the landing then hammered on Jess's door. 'Air raid,' he shouted. 'Mum says to hurry up!' Their five-year old sister Shirley, with whom Jess shared the bed, was already awake and let out a yell as he dashed into the room, grabbed her arm and pulled her from between the sheets. 'Shut up,' he shouted, snatching the first thing he could find and throwing it at her. 'Put that on and hurry up. The siren's gone off.'

They all scrambled down the stairs to where their father, Fred, waited with the front door open and as they ran across the garden to the shelter in the corner, the familiar drone of enemy planes coming in over the Solent filled the air. Within minutes, Ack Ack guns along the seafront went into action as the first stick of bombs whistled past and exploded nearby.

'Blimey that was close, Dad,' Billy said, as a massive explosion shook the ground and the shelter rocked and rattled. The force of the blast lifted the flimsy, makeshift door out of its hole and tossed it into the garden. At the sound of shattering glass, Billy peered through the open gap and could see by the light of the moon and through a thick layer of dust that, although some of its windows were missing, the house was still standing in one piece. He retched as the sickly stench of cordite caught in his throat and made him cough. 'Phew. It stinks out here,' he said. 'An' there's glass *everywhere*.'

When the all clear sounded, they climbed from the shelter and picked their way carefully along the path to the front door, thankful, as they always were after an air raid, that they were still alive.

By this time, Billy no longer felt tired, and hung around listening to his parents talking. They were discussing evacuation.

'I know we've always promised not to send Billy and Jess away,' he heard his mother say, 'but the air raids are getting worse again. Shirley's a bit too young but there's no reason why the other two can't go.'

'I don't like the idea of it, Doris,' his father replied, 'but I'll think about it.'

Billy didn't care whether his father thought about it or not, he didn't want to go away and live with strangers and if they tried to do it, he would refuse. Even run away if necessary. He'd heard the evacuee stories about the beatings, the bullying, and how some people were using the children as skivvies. Many parents had brought their children home because of this. One such boy in his class still had the marks on his legs where his host mother had beaten him just for refusing to scrub her kitchen floor before he went to school.

Billy left them talking about where and when he and Jess might go, then went up the stairs to his bedroom and climbed into bed, where, for some time, he lay awake making his plans – just in case. Eventually, he fell into a restless, dream-filled sleep where an old woman with her hair tied back in a bun and a face like a pickled walnut, poked and prodded him with a broom handle as he scrubbed her kitchen floor.

Chapter Two

A Piece of Shrapnel

Billy loved breakfast on Sunday when, as a special treat, they each had their egg ration, fried, with a thick slice of toast. He cut his toast into fingers and dipped them into the dark orange yolk, smacking his lips together at the rich flavour of the egg while thinking of the conversation he'd listened in to about evacuation. He would *not* go, and they'd be sorry if they tried to make him.

'I went for a walk before any of you were up,' his father said, 'to see where that bomb fell during the night. It landed in the park – on the playing fields. No one hurt but plenty of windows gone and roofs damaged. And there's a huge crater where the football pitch used to be.'

Billy stopped eating and his ears pricked up. There might be some good pickings for his shrapnel collection there.

Fred Parkin held up a copy of the Portsmouth Evening News. 'I read this after you'd gone to bed last night, Doris,' he said to his wife. 'There's an advert in it for a cottage, and I wonder if it would be any good to us.' He read it aloud across the table:

'Small cottage to let for a minimum of one year, in nice woodland position, twelve miles' from Portsmouth. Might suit a family who want to escape from the air raids. Please write to Miss Clarice Foster for an appointment to view'.

The address given was at Horndean – a small village on the other side of Portsmouth. Billy cheered up a bit. It might not be so bad if they could all move away together, instead of him and Jess having to go to strangers where they would probably be unhappy and homesick.

As soon as breakfast was over, he left his mother writing to Miss Foster. 'I'm just goin' to help dad board up the broken windows,' he said. 'Then I'm goin' to the park.'

When he and his father had finished, Billy decided to go and have a look at the bomb crater. A few other boys from the neighbourhood, including Dave, had already gathered around the hole in the ground and the search for shrapnel had begun. Billy found several small pieces before coming across the very thing he was looking for – a large nugget, roughly four inches in diameter and weighing, he guessed, about half a pound. He felt the rough warmth of it in the palm of his hand.

'What d'you think you're doin' with that?'

He jumped, startled as a familiar voice brought him round to face local bully Brendan Trapper and some of his friends. Billy's hand tightened over the piece of metal. 'What's it to you then?' he said, with a lot more courage than he felt. Trapper was in his class at school, and twice the size of Billy. Not only that, the bully had recently switched his unwelcome attentions from the Larcombe brothers who had moved to Dorset, to Billy.

'Give it'ere!' Trapper held out a fat, grubby hand for Billy's precious lump of shrapnel. Billy stood firm. He was in a spot of bother here. If he let Trapper have the shrapnel, he'd probably get away with nothing more than a black eye for having found it first. If he refused, he would likely be beaten up and then thrown into the bomb crater. A vision of him lying injured at the bottom of that enormous hole swam before his eyes. Supposing he died before anyone could get him out, and if he hadn't died, how badly injured would he be? He might never be able to walk again. Worse still, what if the Corporation men came along to fill it in and didn't notice he was in there? He'd be buried alive. His hands were shaking, his mouth dry but he was not going to give in to Trapper's bullying. He stared straight into his enemy's eyes.

'Get lost, Trapper.'

Trapper's face turned a nasty shade of red. He wasn't used to anyone standing up to him.

'I *said*, give it'ere.'

'No.'

Trapper edged closer and Billy could see the beads of sweat standing out on his spotty face. By this time, a crowd of local boys and girls had gathered to watch the fun. They all knew Brendan Trapper, and were amazed to see Billy standing up to the notorious bully. Not one of them would dare try to get the better of him.

'You deaf or somethin'?' Trapper looked as mad as a half-dead wasp.

'No. An' you're not havin' it, Fatso.'

Billy jumped as Trapper's finger jabbed into his chest. 'That's one I owe you for callin' me names,' he said.

The silent, watching crowd suddenly woke up and Dave Spiller shouted, 'Go on, Billy – give 'im what-for!' Everybody cheered as Billy handed the piece of shrapnel to his friend and took a swing at the bully. He missed his target and lost his footing when Trapper's fist caught him under his chin. Trapper laughed as Billy went sprawling among the remains of the goal posts uprooted by the bomb last night. The spectators cheered and clapped when he scrambled to his feet and, as he saw Trapper's fist coming for him again, sidestepped out of the way. Trapper, a look of surprise on his face, waved his arms in the air and then lost his balance and disappeared over the edge of the crater into the hole below. Everyone surged forward to watch as he tried to get to his feet.

'I'll get you for this, Parkin,' he yelled, unable to untwist himself from where he had fallen. 'Just you wait an' see if I don't!'

Billy peered over the side of the hole and laughed. 'Serves you right,' he shouted back. 'You oughta keep that big mouth of yours shut.'

'We can't leave him down there,' one of Trapper's friends said, giving Billy a dark look. 'I'll go and get help.'

Once all the excitement was over, most of Billy's supporters hung around, waiting to see what would happen next. Trapper's friend had found a policeman, and Billy watched as the constable pushed his bicycle across the park and peered into the crater. 'Nothing I can do here. It's a Fire Brigade job,' he said and sped off on his bicycle to make a telephone call.

It took half an hour, with the help of the Fire Brigade, to lift Trapper out of the hole. When he finally surfaced, an ambulance took him away to the local hospital to see how bad his injuries were.

As they left the park, Billy asked Dave for the piece of shrapnel. He held it up to examine it. 'I've made Trapper look like an idiot 'cos of this,' he said. 'Maybe made him break a leg or somethin', an' he'll get his own back on me for that.'

Chapter Three

Tragedy

That night, during another air raid, a stick of bombs fell on some of the little streets close to Eastland School. The next morning, when Billy arrived, he could only stand and stare, open-mouthed at the gaping holes and piles of rubble where once had stood a row of houses. A cloud of dust hung in the air and he covered his eyes with his hands, unable to look at the remains of where Dave had lived.

The headmaster greeted the children at the gates. 'There will be no school today,' he said, waving a hand over the debris-strewn playground. 'All the windows on this side are broken and there's glass everywhere. You'd better go home and come back tomorrow.' His voice broke as he went on to explain that several pupils and their families had lost their lives in the bombing. 'I'll be posting a list of casualties at the gate as soon as I know who they are.'

Billy raised his hand. 'Please, sir,' he said. 'D'you know what happened to Dave Spiller?'

The headmaster shook his head. 'I don't know any more than you, Parkin,' he said. 'Run along home and we'll see what tomorrow brings.'

When school re-opened the following morning, Billy learned that several boys and girls from each class were absent. 'There will be no lessons today,' the headmaster announced at assembly. 'Each of you will be given tasks to help with the clearing up of your own classroom. Tasks that will, I hope, help keep your minds on something other than this terrible tragedy.'

An eerie silence hovered over the empty desks of the missing children and neither Billy nor anyone else could concentrate on what they were supposed to be doing. 'Has anyone seen Dave Spiller?' he kept asking first one, and then another of his classmates, but no one had. At playtime, he joined one of the many groups of children in the playground who wanted to do nothing but wait around for news of their friends.

Later that afternoon, the teachers assembled their pupils in the hall, where the children stood in silence as the headmaster read out the names of those who had died. Seven boys and five girls had lost their lives, among them Billy's friend Dave, and Brendan Trapper, whose injuries the previous afternoon had amounted to no more than a few bruises. In the dusty hall, with its broken windows temporarily patched up with bits of board, pupils and teachers cried together for the lost children. They said prayers, sung a hymn, and Miss Bancroft, the English teacher then gave a short speech before dismissing the assembly. 'Go home, now,' she said, 'and try not to feel too sad for your lost friends. We believe it all happened so suddenly that none of them would have known anything at all.' She paused to blow her nose and compose herself. 'You will never forget them but, in time, there will be others to take their place.'

As he left school, Billy paused at the gate to look at what was left of Dave's house opposite. The road had been cordoned off and several policemen stood guard as workmen sifted through the rubble. The terraced houses lay flattened, what remained of their contents scattered over a wide area. A pile of rubble covered the roof of the Anderson shelter at the side of Dave's house but otherwise it was untouched. Billy couldn't understand why Dave's family hadn't gone to the shelter, although only the other day he'd said that they didn't always bother, especially in the middle of the night.

'My mum reckons the worst of the raids are over,' he'd said.

Billy turned his head away, unable to watch as one of the men uncovered a baby's pushchair, lifted it up and placed it on the top of a pile of other bits and pieces of salvage. He recognised that pushchair. It had belonged to Dave's little sister, Betty. He brushed tears from his eyes as he tried to imagine what had happened. How did Dave die? Had he been asleep when the bombs fell? Or awake and crushed beneath the debris; crying out for help, with no one able to reach him in time? And what about two-year-old Betty, and their mum? Billy noticed two men loading a covered stretcher into an ambulance. That meant they were still finding bodies. He felt a hand on his shoulder and turned to stare into the kindly face of a policeman. 'Run along, sonny,' the man said. 'This is no place for you.'

Billy wiped his nose in his sleeve and pointed to the ruins of Dave's house. 'My best friend lived there,' he said.

'I'm sorry to hear that but your friend wouldn't have known anything.'

Billy wasn't sure whether or not to believe this. How did this man know? He wandered off, thinking about Dave, crushed to death by all that rubble, and buried beneath the ruins of his own home. He would miss him. They had done everything together for seven years, ever since starting school in the same class. Football in the park, picnics on the beach, Saturday morning pictures at the Regal and swapping stamps - all gone. He remembered last Saturday when they'd gone to the Regal to see a Roy Roger's film and Dave had given him half his week's sweet ration.

He found an empty shop, went into the doorway and cried for a while, then brushed away the tears from his eyes in case he should meet up with someone he knew. He didn't want anyone to think he was a cissy. Then he gave a thought to Brendan Trapper who, even though he'd been a bully, hadn't deserved to die either.

As he turned to take a shortcut through the park, he saw Jess sitting on a bench and stopped to ask why she was crying. 'My friend, Sally died in the raid,' she said. 'We were playing on the swings last Saturday, and now she'd dead. She was ever so pretty,' Jess went on, tears streaming down her face, 'with lovely long hair, and she was my best friend. Her mum and brother were killed too.'

'So was Dave Spiller,' Billy said. 'My best friend, I mean. He was killed too, *and* his mum and baby sister.'

Jess stopped crying. 'Oh, *no*, Billy,' she said, 'not *Dave*?'

'Yep.' Billy sniffed into his handkerchief. 'Where's Sally's dad?' he said.

'He's away, in the Army.'

'Dave's is in the Airforce. I think he's in Malta somewhere.'

Jess shook her head. 'Why do we have to have wars, Billy?'

Billy thought about that. ''It's 'cos of greedy men like Hitler who want to take over the world,' he said. 'Yeah, that's what it is, I think.' He offered her his grubby handkerchief and waited until she'd dried her eyes. 'Least, that's what our teacher says.'

They sat there for several minutes, not saying anything and then she gave him a watery smile. He pulled her to her feet.

'C'mon, let's go an' see what mum's made us for tea,' he said, trying to lift her spirits, although the thought of eating anything at all made him feel sick. 'Cheese on toast, I hope.' He swallowed on the painful lump in his throat. 'I won't ever, *ever* say I'm not scared of air raids again,' he promised.

Chapter Four

Railway Cottage

Billy missed Dave so much. He had other pals of
course but they weren't the same and whenever he
thought of his friend, his heart felt like a lump of lead
in his chest and he found it hard to fight back the
tears. Sometimes, if he happened to be indoors, he'd
go up to his bedroom where no one could see him
and have a good cry. Then there were the nightmares
when he could hear Dave screaming for help but he,
Billy, couldn't get to him. In the dream, Billy tried
desperately with his bare hands, to pull all the rubble
away from where he thought Dave's voice might be
coming from. But for every brick he moved, a pile of
others would take its place until a great mound of
rubble, as tall as Billy himself, covered the place
where Dave lay. Then unseen hands from behind
would pull Billy away and tell him to go home.
'You'll get hurt, sonny,' a man's voice would say.
'There's nothing you can do.' Then Billy would
wake up, thrashing about the bed in a cold sweat and
have to run to the lavatory.

He wondered if he'd ever get over Dave and
the way he had died, and almost hated his mother
when she would not allow him to go to the funeral.

'It's no place for you,' Billy, she said. 'You'll
only get upset.'

'I *want* to go,' he argued but despite his
pleading, she wouldn't give in. On the morning of
the funeral, he skipped school and went to the park

where he and Dave had often played football. There, he sat there for a while, thinking about his friend, then wandered over to where the exit came out opposite the Regal, and stood looking across the road at the boards advertising the forthcoming pictures. "Tarzan's Secret Treasure, with Johnny Weissmuller", he read. Dave had been looking forward to that. Billy caught the toe of his boot in an old tin can and kicked it along the road. He no longer cared about moving to the country. What difference did it make now that Dave was no longer around.

A week after Billy's mother had written to Miss Foster, a letter arrived to say that the following Saturday would be the best time to view the cottage. 'She's enclosed some directions, and says she hopes the cottage will be suitable for us,' she said.

On the day, instead of letting him stay in bed until half-past eight, as he usually did on a Saturday, Billy's mother woke him up at seven o'clock. He moaned when she ordered him to wash, dress and have breakfast and to "look sharp about it," as they had a bus to catch. Jess and Shirley were already up and ready to go.

'Why do *I* have to go to Horndean?' he wanted to know. 'And where's dad?'

'You're not staying here all day on your own, and your father has to work on Saturdays now, so get up and move yourself.'

He dragged himself out of bed and at half-past eight, in a bad temper, boarded a number forty Southdown bus with his mother and sisters. As it chugged up the slopes of Portsdown Hill, leaving the City of Portsmouth behind in a blanket of fog, he began to cheer up a bit. In a way, a move to the cottage would turn out to be best; otherwise, for him and Jess it would mean evacuation.

'Why do we have to move?' Jess, who hated buses, whispered to Billy. 'The smell of petrol makes me feel sick, and these wooden seats are hard. Anyway, the air raids aren't as bad now as they used to be.'

'Mum thinks she knows best,' Billy said, still feeling annoyed with her for dragging him along. 'I suppose it might be nice though, not to have to get out of bed and run to the shelter.'

Jess agreed with that. They all hated the Anderson. Damp, cold and with no room to move, it was full of spiders. Big, black and hairy, they were all over the place and you just had to shut your eyes and let them crawl over you. Even Billy didn't like them. His father had made the shelter as comfortable as he could but had not been able to do anything about the water seeping in or the sour smell of clay soil, which made everyone feel sick. '*Anything* would be better than that,' Billy pointed out to Jess. 'And do you really want to be evacuated?' he said, ''cos that's what'll happen to us. I heard mum and dad talking the other night'.

'You've been ear wigging again,' Jess said, using the expression their mother did whenever she caught Billy listening in.

The conductor moved along the bus and had a word with their mother. 'You wanted to know when we reached Catherton Lane,' he said, ruffling Shirley's fair hair. She poked her tongue out at him as far as it would go. 'It's the next stop.'

Doris Parkin thanked him, gave Shirley's hand a sharp smack for being so rude, and rose from her seat, ushering the children to the front of the bus. It dropped them off at the corner of a narrow road and Billy looked over his mother's shoulder at directions on the sheet of paper Miss Foster had sent her.

'It's this way,' he said, pointing downhill towards some woods.

As they made their way in what they thought was the right direction, a mild spring wind whistled gently through the telegraph wires overhead, and sent banks of low, grey rain clouds scurrying across a leaden sky. It reminded Billy of the day he and Jess had been machine-gunned, and a cold shiver ran down his spine. About half-a-mile on, he stopped. 'I've got a blister come up on my heel,' he said.

Shirley started grizzling. 'Are we nearly there?' she moaned. 'My legs hurt.'

'Well, I think we're lost,' Jess put in.

'I think we should go back,' their mother said, as they came upon a lane to the left, which was arrowed on Miss Foster's sketch. On the corner, a mud-spattered nameplate, half-hidden by a hedge, leaned crookedly to one side.

'This can't be it,' Billy said. 'It's just a dirt track.' He moved over to see if he could read what was on it. 'What's it called?'

'Woodsmoke Lane.'

'Well, this *is* it.'

'It can't be.'

Billy laughed. 'It *is*, Mum.' He saw the worried expression on her face and wondered what she was going to do next. Miss Foster had not said anything about a mud track. 'Let's go on anyway,' he said, taking the lead. 'We might as well.'

The lane twisted and turned through dense woodland covered in a carpet of early primroses and wild violets. As they ploughed their way up towards the top, thick, slimy mud sucked at their shoes so that they could hardly keep them on their feet. Shirley almost walked out of hers, and Billy couldn't stop laughing until his mother threatened to box his ears. On either side of the track, an odd assortment of homes sat dotted among the trees. Wisps of smoke curled upwards from lopsided chimneys of ramshackle shacks and caravans, filling the air with the smell of burning wood.

'I love that smell,' Billy said, taking a deep breath. 'I 'spect that's why it's called Woodsmoke Lane.' It all looked a bit shabby. 'Do people really live in those places?' he asked his mother.

'It looks as if they do,' she replied, 'though goodness knows how they manage.'

They eventually came to a wooden gate with the name Railway Cottage painted on it. As his gaze travelled along the path leading to the front door Billy saw, not a cottage, but a dark green coloured railway carriage with a verandah running along the full width of the front, and what looked like an extra room built onto the end.

'We are *not* going in there,' his mother said from behind.

'Yes we are, Mum. Come on.' Billy was already halfway up the path and having come all this way, wanted to see what it was like inside. The front door opened and an elderly woman who, Billy thought, looked like a stick insect, appeared.

'Good morning,' the stick insect said, extending a bony hand. 'I'm Miss Clarice Foster, and you must be the Parkin family.' She glanced down at four pairs of muddy feet. 'Would you mind very much taking your shoes off before you come in?' They did as she asked and she guided them inside where she introduced them to her twin sister Miss Avril. The two women were dressed in identical black skirts and grey jumpers and looked exactly alike. Both had white hair drawn back in a bun, and feet encased in black boots with, Billy noticed, many buttons down the sides. Miss Avril smiled, shook hands, and then disappeared into the kitchen to put the kettle on.

Billy glanced around the tiny sitting room. It looked quite nice really, if you didn't mind the low, curved ceilings and railway carriage windows, complete with leather straps with which to open them. The furniture looked old, and the carpets a bit threadbare, but it felt cosy. His nose detected the faint smell of mothballs and paraffin and something cooking. Then he spotted a couple of large spiders on the wall and was about to point them out to the girls when he caught his mother's eye, daring him to do any such thing. He grinned at her as she left him and his sisters in the care of Miss Avril, and went with Miss Clarice to view the rest of the cottage.

It had everything they needed, except for a bathroom. Miss Clarice apologised for the tin bath hanging on a nail in the porch, and for the outside lavatory. She lowered her voice. 'But there are chamber pots underneath each bed,' she whispered, 'in case you need to ah, *visit* during the night – as it were.' She offered her visitor a pair of Wellingtons and showed her into the garden where an orchard ran along one side of the home. 'There are red and golden plums,' she said, 'pears, eating apples and Bramley cookers. We also have red and black currant bushes, raspberries, two cherry trees and, in September, the lane is full of blackberries and hazel nuts.' She waved a hand towards a coppice at the end of the garden. 'That belongs to the cottage,' she said. 'Your children will love it.'

Billy stood at the back door and listened. He could hear the two women talking and overheard his mother ask if there were ever any air raids over Horndean. 'We sometimes get air raid warnings,' Miss Clarice said, 'but only the odd, stray German aeroplane trying to find its way home, and nothing worth worrying about. Sometimes though, with the wind in the right direction, it's possible to hear the raids going on over Portsmouth, but that's all.' He moved quickly away from the door when he saw them making their way back to the cottage and pulled a face at Jess when their mother spoilt everything by asking about schools.

'Walking distance for the girls,' Miss Avril said, 'and a bus up on the main road for the seniors.'

'The rent is ten shillings a week, including rates and electricity and you will be welcome to stay as long as you like,' Miss Clarice, who seemed to be in charge of everything, said as she showed them to the door. 'My sister and I live in the New Forest and only use Railway Cottage for holidays, so you may have it until the end of the war if you wish.'

Billy wasn't too sure about his mother agreeing to take the cottage for a year. As they walked down the lane, he thought about the move. New school, new friends; it might be fun, although he'd miss Portsmouth even though there wasn't much left of it now. The blitz two years ago had left the city in ruins. He supposed it would good for them all to get away from that but wondered whether he'd like living out here in the wilds, where there were no parks or Saturday morning picture houses, and he'd have to catch a bus to get to school. He looked at Jess. 'I think it's all right,' he said. 'D'*you* like it?'

Jess looked unhappy. 'I suppose so.'

He pulled at one of Shirley's pigtails. 'No more air raids, Shirley,' he said. 'Now, what d'you think of that?'

They didn't find out what Shirley thought of that because as they reached the main road, Billy saw their bus coming and they had to run the last fifty yards to catch it. As it rattled along the road towards Portsmouth, his mind was still on the move to Horndean. It wouldn't be too bad, he thought. He'd make another friend, although it wouldn't be the same as Dave, who had died in the air raid. Billy would never forget him, but *he* wouldn't be coming back anyway. And it was better than being evacuated, wasn't it? He turned round in his seat to say something to Jess, but she had fallen asleep.

Chapter Five

Moving Day

Billy held up the brown paper carrier by its string handles. 'How am I supposed to get everything in here?' he said to his mother. She had given one each to him, Jess and Shirley, with instructions to fill it only with things that they would really need. A change of underclothing, some spare socks, a flannel, a tin of Eucryl toothpowder and some soap. 'It's nearly full and there's no room for my Meccano.'

'You'll make do with a couple of books and some comics and be satisfied,' she told him. 'There are enough problems with trying to move without you adding to them.'

Fred Parkin had managed to get a day off from the dockyard and, at ten o'clock one sunny, May Saturday morning, the Parkin family, with as many belongings as they could each carry, set off to catch a bus to Horndean.

On the first night at Railway Cottage, Billy couldn't sleep. He tossed and turned in the unfamiliar bed until sometime in the middle of the night, he decided to get himself a drink of water. He slipped out of bed, went through to the kitchen, stood at the window and looked out at a black, bottomless pit of darkness. In Portsmouth, although there was the blackout, you could always see *something* at night, and it was never as dark as this. From somewhere in the depths of the copse at the end of the garden, an assortment of animal noises echoed through the trees. An owl hooted, and Billy could hear the snuffling and scratching of what the girl next door told him later was probably a badger. He shivered, partly from cold and partly from fear of the unknown and then went back to bed and buried his head under the covers.

The next day, as he left Railway Cottage to explore the village to find out where the shops were for his mother, he met a boy of about his own age. 'I'm Danny Palmer,' the boy said, holding out one hand, like a grown-up. All arms, legs and freckles, and wearing glasses, he looked like one of the tawny owls from The Boys' Bumper Book of Birds, given to Billy for his twelfth birthday in January.

'Would you like to join the Woodlarks?' Danny asked. 'It's a club, formed to raise money for the war effort.'

'I don't know,' Billy said. 'Depends what I'd have to do.'

'Why don't you come to the next meeting?' the other boy suggested. He pointed to an old shack across the lane. 'That's old Jethro Quirk's place,' he said, 'and I live behind it. The meeting's at ten o'clock next Saturday morning in my garden.'

'Well ... I ...'

'If you have any brothers or sisters, they can come if they're over ten.'

'My sister Jess is nearly eleven.'

'Well, bring *her* then,' Danny said. 'We need lots of help with a book collection.'

'Book collection?'

'Yes. I'll tell you all about it on Saturday. Go to go now. My mum's waiting for me.'

Before Billy could make up his mind, Danny shot across the lane and disappeared down the side of Jethro Quirk's shack.

'D'you want to go?' Billy said to Jess, after he'd told her about the Woodlark club.

'Yes,' Jess said. 'But we're not taking Shirley, and I bet our mum won't let me go if we don't.'

'We can't take her anyway, she's too young. But *I'll* ask mum if you like.'

'Just this once,' their mother said. 'You and Jess are not going to make a habit of leaving her on her own with no one to play with.'

Billy made a face.

The following Saturday morning, ignoring all the foot stamping and tears from Shirley, Billy and Jess set off without her. There was no mistaking where Jethro Quirke lived. A piece of old board, propped up at the side of his front door said, in large, black painted lettering that, "Mr. Jethro A. Quirke, retired Master Builder lives here." Billy sniggered as they crept down the path at the side. 'I wonder what kind of things he built,' he said, glancing sideways at the tumbledown shack the old man called home. The cottage where Danny lived was easy to find and when he and Jess arrived, they found him waiting in the garden with a girl about the same age as Jess. She had auburn hair that tumbled in curls over her shoulders, dark blue eyes and a wide smile for Billy and Jess.

'This is Meg,' Danny said. 'She lives next door to you.'

Billy looked around. This was supposed to be a meeting but there was no sign of anyone else. 'This is my sister, Jess,' he said. 'Where are all the others?'

Danny apologised for absent members. 'They're all busy helping their dads today,' he said. 'So we'll have to manage without them.'

'How many members are there?' Billy wanted to know.

'There's me, Meg and another two besides you and Jess.'

Billy smiled. 'Six? That's not much of a club, is it,' he said.

Danny threw him a dirty look.

They seated themselves on the lawn. 'The Woodlarks,' he began, 'is a sort of club formed by me and another boy, Sam, to raise money for the war effort. So far, we have donated ten pounds and eight shillings to the Spitfire Fund, and a few small sums to other worthy causes. We want to do something really wizard for the Aid to Russia Fund too, which is run by the Prime Minister's wife, Mrs Churchill.' His eyes rested on Billy and Jess. 'But first, there is an urgent need for old books so I thought we'd do that next. Would you be able to go around collecting?'

'Go around where?' Billy wanted to know.

'The houses in the village, of course.' Danny sounded annoyed.

'Our dad won't like that,' Billy said.

'You can ask him, can't you?'

'I suppose so.' Billy wasn't sure what his dad would say about knocking on the doors of people they didn't know.

'My Auntie Dorothy is in charge of the village hall,' Danny said, 'and she says we can take them there to be sorted before they go away to be pulped.'

'What happens to them after that?' Billy loved reading just about anything and it seemed a funny sort of thing to do to perfectly good books. He didn't like this Danny much. He spoke in a lah-de-dah voice and seemed to think a lot of himself.

'I don't know,' Danny admitted, 'but she said that the pulp can be used to make mortar shell carriers and other important things like that.' He handed a clean sheet of paper and a pencil to Meg. 'Here's what we do then. We'll go in pairs and so that we don't knock on the same doors twice, Meg will sort out which roads each couple will do. There is,' he went on, 'one place that is strictly out of bounds. Crows Nest Cottage in Potters Lane, where Perizada the Mad Witch lives. Set one foot in her garden and you'll be in trouble.'

'A witch?' Billy said. 'No such things as witches.' He was beginning to think that it was all a bit silly, knocking on doors asking for things. And witches?

Meg spoke up for the first time. 'Well,' she said, 'the postman says she has a pond full of frogs in the front garden and three black cats that spit at anyone who goes to the front door. Not only that, there's always a large black crow perched on the chimney pot.'

'That doesn't mean she's a witch,' Billy said.

'She wanders around the garden after dark in a long white gown and talks to the moon. And she sings to the bats as well.'

He laughed. 'What a load of old rubbish. Have *you* ever seen her do any of that?'

'No.'

'Well then.'

'Excuse me,' Danny said. 'Could we get on with the meeting? I want to have a game of football before dinner. I think we should start collecting on the Monday after next, as there isn't any school that week. We'll sort the books on the Tuesday and take them to the village hall on Wednesday. You can't miss it – it's right next to the brewery.'

They all agreed and the meeting finished with Meg offering to ask her dad, who did a bit of painting in his spare time, to do some posters.

Billy and Jess strolled back to Railway Cottage with Meg. 'Would you like to go for a walk tomorrow?' she asked. 'I could show you where Perizada the Mad Witch lives if you like.'

'All right,' Billy replied. 'But we'll have to bring Shirley.'

'Shirley?'

'Yes, our little sister. She's five.'

'I wish *I* had a sister,' Meg said. 'What's she like?'

'She looks like a little angel, with golden hair and blue eyes, but she's really a spoilt little beast. Our mum expects us to take her everywhere with us,' Billy said.

'I think you're lucky,' Meg said, as she turned into her gateway. 'See you tomorrow, then. About ten o'clock.'

Billy and Jess went indoors. 'Do you believe that story about a witch?' Jess asked Billy.

'Load of old rubbish, if you ask me,' he said.

'What d'you think of Meg?'

'She's all right, I suppose. 'For a *girl*.'

'I like her,' Jess said. 'She looks a bit like my friend, Sally, who was killed in that air raid.'

Chapter Six

Looking Around

The following morning, Billy, Jess and Shirley climbed over the fence into Meg's garden where she was waiting for them by the door of an old wooden shed. 'I want to show you something before we go,' she said, leading the way into a dingy, musty-smelling building where, in a large basket lined with a blanket, a black and white cat lay sleeping with her kittens.

Billy stood aside as Jess and Shirley crouched down for a closer look. 'I don't want to see them,' he said. 'I don't like cats. They're spiteful and dig you with their claws or want to sit on your lap and then you have to stroke them.' He pulled a face. 'Their bodies quiver when they purr and it makes me feel all shivery.' He preferred dogs to cats but his mother didn't like them so there was no chance of him ever having one of his own.

The girls were there for ages fawning over the kittens, and he was impatient to get going. 'Come on,' he shouted presently, 'never mind about cats. It'll be dinnertime before we get started.'

'D'you think mum would let us have a kitten?' Jess asked Billy.

'I hope not,' he said. 'I *hate* them.'

Potters Lane was at the bottom of a long steep hill, bordered on one side by a dense coppice and on the other, an open field full of cows. A notice by the gate read "BEWARE OF THE BULL." Billy teased Jess about the red coat she was wearing. 'They don't like red,' he said. 'It makes them mad. He'll chase you down the lane and stick one of those big horns in your belly.'

'Don't take any notice of *him*,' Meg said. 'Bruno's really quite a friendly bull. Sometimes he comes over to the gate to see what's going on but he won't hurt you.'

Bruno stopped chewing grass and started pawing the ground while staring at them in a way that Jess thought was definitely *not* very friendly. Then he began to trot towards them, his eyes fixed on her coat, and she fled, with Shirley following close behind.

'What a pair of ninnies you two are,' Billy said when he and Meg caught them up. He looked around at the posh houses and bungalows on either side of Potters Lane, 'Well, never mind about the bull. Where does this Perizada the Mad Witch live then?'

Meg told them to follow her, and took the lead until they came to a corner on the left where, behind a rickety wooden gate, a gravel drive led to an ivy-covered thatched cottage set against a backdrop of pine trees. The front garden, a tangle of overgrown bushes, almost hid the pond, which Meg had said was full of frogs.

'I don't see any,' Billy said, still not believing all that nonsense about a witch. 'If she keeps frogs, where *are* they then?'

'Don't you know *anything*?' Meg said. 'Frogs are very good at camouflaging themselves to blend in gwith their surroundings and it's not always easy to see them. *Everyone* knows that. You wouldn't be able to see them from here anyway.'

'All right clever sticks. I suppose you think just because you live in the country, you know everything about nature.'

'I know more than you do.'

'Don't be stupid. Girls don't know *anything*.'

On the front steps, three black cats lay curled up, fast asleep in the warm spring sunshine. 'Well, at least it's true about the cats, but I don't see any crows up there,' he said, pointing to a tall, twisted chimney, which looked like a stick of barley sugar. He noticed an old bicycle, with a basket on the front, leaning against the wall by the front door. 'And I always thought that witches rode on broomsticks, not bikes.' He could tell by Meg's face that she was getting annoyed with him for making fun of her.

'It was a waste of time bringing *you* here,' she said. 'Anyway, you are not allowed to call here when you do your book collections.'

'We'll see,' Billy said. Nothing would stop him calling on Perizada the Mad Witch, no matter what anyone said. He wanted to find out if what the others had told him was true or, just as he thought, a load of stupid, made-up stories.

Meg was just about to show them around the local churchyard when the air raid siren went off and Shirley let out such an ear-piercing scream that it brought an old lady running from her cottage to see what all the commotion was about. 'Goodness gracious me,' she exclaimed, wiping floury hands in her pinafore, 'what in the world is the matter?' She was a very large lady with a mop of grey, unruly hair, and lots of whisker-covered chins that wobbled in all directions. She shook her head in amazement at the noise this strange child was making.

'She's scared of the air raids,' Billy said. 'We've just come out from Portsmouth to get away from them. We didn't think there would be any here.'

Shirley would not stop screaming as she stamped her feet and wet her knickers. The old lady moved closer to her and wagged a podgy finger in her face 'I think we've heard just about enough from you, young lady,' she said, silencing the screaming child with a fierce look from eyes that glittered like two black marbles. 'Yes, we do sometimes get air raid warnings but German planes don't come this far and have never dropped anything around here, so just you stop making all that noise.' She turned to Billy. 'Whereabouts do you live?'

'Just round the corner, in Woodsmoke Lane,' he said.

'Would that be Railway Cottage?'

'Yes.'

'Ah, the new people.' Her voice took on a more kindly tone. 'Well,' she advised, 'I should take her home and get her out of those wet things before she catches her death of cold.' She waddled towards her front door. 'My name is Mrs Lavender Baggit,' she called over her shoulder. 'Tell your mother that I'll come by and see her sometime when I have a minute.'

Billy promised to pass on the message.

When they reached their gate, he kept on walking. 'I'm fed up with girls' he said to Jess. 'I'm goin' to have a look round. Tell mum I won't be long.'

Chapter Seven

An Enemy

The stone hit Billy between the shoulder blades with such force that his knees buckled and he found himself lying face down in the dirt. From what seemed a long way off, a voice came out at him through the trees. 'Git back to Pompey where you came from,' it said. 'We don't want 'vacuees 'ere, so clear off, Pompey Fleabag.' Billy tried to get up but the last thing he remembered before slipping into a black hole of unconsciousness was the face of a man with a ginger beard, who lifted him up and carried him along the lane towards home.

When he came round, he was on his own bed, his mother hovering over him with a glass of something that looked like muddy water. 'Sit up and drink this,' she said. 'It'll make you feel better.'

'Ugh,' he said, spitting some of it out, 'it's horrible.' He winced at the pain in his back, and looked at the man who was standing by the bed writing something in a notebook.

'This is Doctor Bainbridge,' Billy's mother said. 'And wasn't it lucky that the doctor happened to be passing when, whoever it was, decided to throw that great big stone at you.'

Billy's head felt all woozy. He could see his father outlined in the doorway, and tried to listen as some strange woman wittered on about how naughty her George was to have done such a dreadful thing. She was going on about George's dad not being here to give him a belting when he deserved one. Billy's mother asked where the missing father was.

'He's in the Navy,' the woman said. 'I'm Mrs Bunn, and live with my boy in a caravan down the lane. His dad's been away for months and we don't even know where he is. George misses him something terrible.' Mrs Bunn peered into the room where Billy, with his mother's help, was trying to swing his legs round so that he could stand up. 'I'll fetch George,' she said, 'and make him say how sorry he is.' She put her hands up to her face as Billy wobbled to his feet. 'Oh my goodness,' she exclaimed, 'the poor boy can't even stand up. I'll give my boy a good hiding for this, make no mistake about that.'

When she had gone, Doctor Bainbridge handed Billy's mother a bottle of the muddy-looking water. 'That will ease the pain for him,' he said, 'but I don't think there's any damage done although he'll feel bruised for a few days.' She thanked him, offered him a cup of tea and asked how much she owed him. 'Very kind of you ma'am,' he said, gathering up his bag, 'but my wife was expecting me home a good half an hour ago, so I'd better be off. And you don't owe me anything. I'm just thankful I happened to be passing and caught the culprit.'

By the end of the week, the dark purple bruise had faded to yellow, thanks to Billy's mother bathing it daily with witch hazel, and the muddy medicine she forced down his throat. Mrs Bunn was as good as her word and dragged the unwilling George along to apologise, which he did under protest. A frail looking boy with fair hair and a pale face; the only colourful thing about him was a pair of large, red ears that stuck out like jug handles. 'I'm sorry. I didn't mean it,' he mumbled as his mother looked on. But when she turned away to speak to Billy's mother, he pushed his face up close to Billy's. 'You watch out, Fleabag, 'cos there's more of the same to come,' he said in a whisper so that his mother couldn't hear. 'You'll see.'

Billy began to wonder if Brendan Trapper, in the guise of George Bunn, had come back to haunt him, then told himself not to be so daft. There were no such things as ghosts – or witches for that matter.

When he thought about it, he wasn't sure whether he liked Horndean or not. 'It's a queer place,' he said to Jess, 'with some strange people living in it. They do funny things, like standing at their front gates, whispering to their neighbours. Whenever I go down to the village I see them, and I don't like the way they watch me closely when I'm in the Co-op as if I'm goin' to pinch somethin'. I don't remember seeing people in Chessell Road standing about like that, minding other people's business, do you, Jess?'

'You're making that up, Billy,' Jess said. 'Everyone's been nice to me.'

He spent the next weekend searching for a suitable set of wheels with which to make a trolley for transporting the books. An old dolls pram behind the shed was just the thing and he found a couple of wooden tomato boxes which, with a little bit of adjustment fitted on the chassis perfectly. On Sunday, his father gave him a hand to put it together and, with a long piece of rope fixed to the front with which to pull the contraption along, it was all ready for the next day. He already had a list of the places from Meg, that he and Jess were to call on for their books and he was pleased to see that it included Potters Lane. Meg reminded him that he wasn't to call on Perizada the mad witch.

Billy gave her a devilish smile. He didn't care what anyone said; no one was going to tell him who he should, or should not call on. 'I'll please myself,' he told Jess. 'It's nothing to do with this Meg, Danny Palmer or anyone else.

Chapter Eight

Perizada the Mad Witch

Billy complained about having to take Shirley with them book- collecting. 'She'll get in the way,' he grumbled, but their mother insisted.

'If she doesn't go then neither will you and Jess,' she said, and that was that.

'It's not fair,' he said when they set off and were out of earshot. 'I don't see why we should always have to take her with us everywhere we go.' He caught hold of Shirley's arm and squeezed it hard. 'And don't you *dare* start screaming your head off if the air raid siren goes.'

Shirley poked her tongue out and shook herself free. 'I'll tell mummy you pinched me,' she said, stamping her foot. 'Just you wait and see.'

'Please yourself, tell-tit,' Billy said.

Billy suggested they start in Woodsmoke Lane. 'We can dump the first lot of books at home before we do Potters,' he said, 'then carry on after dinner.' He knew it would be pie and chips today, and he wasn't going to miss *that*.

A lady dressed all in black answered the door to the first home they called at and when Billy explained why they were collecting books, she invited them in to take whatever they needed from a huge bookcase. 'My brother was a soldier,' she told them, 'and these belonged to him but he won't be coming back from the war and I've no use for them.' Her eyes filled with tears. 'I know he'd be only too pleased to see them used to help the war effort,' she said, showing them a photograph of a young, handsome man in the uniform of an army officer. 'He was at Dunkirk you see and the Germans blew up the little rescue boat he was on, or so I was told by another soldier who saw it happen.'

Billy didn't feel happy about taking things that belonged to a dead soldier, and some of the books, with their leather bindings and gold leaf might be worth quite a lot of money. His nose detected a damp, musty smell. He took a book down from the case and looked inside to find its pages covered in spots of mildew and rust marks where damp had attacked the cover and turned it green. Even if they were all like this, it was still a shame to turn them into pulp. 'I'm glad that our dad is too old to fight in the war,' he said to Jess, as they loaded them onto the cart.

By dinnertime they had finished Woodsmoke Lane. Billy looked at the pile of books in the cart. There were about thirty and he wondered how they were going to manage to take them all to the Avenue tomorrow. Then they had to take them to the village hall on Wednesday. His back ached and he was beginning to wish they had never agreed to do this. Besides, collecting books wasn't very exciting and he wanted to go off and do something more interesting. They unloaded the cart onto the verandah and went indoors for their dinner. Shirley, who hadn't stopped complaining about her legs aching, announced that she did not want to go with them again.

Billy smothered his pie and chips in sauce and tucked in. 'Good riddance,' he said.

There were fewer homes in Potters Lane and not as many people wanted to part with their books, so by the time they reached the bottom, the cart was only half-full. Billy went to push open the gate of the Mad Witch's cottage, but Jess stood in his way. 'You're not allowed to go in there,' she whispered.

'Who says so? And what are you whispering for?' He pushed past her and went into the front garden. 'I'm going to knock on her door,' he said. As he picked his way along the weed-covered path, he sensed that someone was watching him. He felt a bit scared now and wished he'd not been so cocky but if he turned back to Jess and the safety of the lane, she would laugh at him and call him a cissy. He reached the front door. The three black cats slept quietly in the porch, but as he approached they woke up, sprang to their feet and with backs arched, hissed and spat at him, their yellow-green eyes following his every move. He backed away from them and tugged at the black, iron bell-pull.

The door opened slowly, as if someone had been standing behind it waiting, and he found himself staring into the pale face of a tall, thin woman dressed in a purple robe. Her long, black hair hung like a pair of curtains to her waist, and she had a large, hooked nose. Billy looked into the greenest pair of eyes he'd ever seen. Except for the absence of a pointed hat, she *did* look like a witch. No wonder that was what the villagers called her.

She fixed him with a stare. 'Well, boy, what is it you want?' she said, in a strange, soft sort of accent.

'I'm …we're…' Billy had presented their mission so many times and now words escaped him. 'We're collecting books.' He pointed back to the lane where Jess waited with the cart. 'It's for the war effort,' he said. 'They mash them up an' then make mortar shells with them.'

'Do they really? Well, you'd better come in,' she said, beckoning him with a long finger.

He knew he shouldn't go with her. How often had his mother warned all of them about not having anything to do with strangers? She led him into a large room, its whitewashed walls covered with shelves on which sat rows of bottles and jars. He could see bunches of dried plants hanging from a beam across the ceiling, and a black iron pot containing a bubbling liquid, suspended on chains over an open a fire. The pungent smell stung his nostrils and made his eyes water. If only he had listened to Jess and not come here.

'See up there,' she said, making him jump as she pointed to a cupboard in the corner. 'Them's all the books I have and they belonged to my mother.' She invited him to sit on a stool by the fire. 'I can't read you see, but when I do want to make my potions and lotions, the pictures in them books tells me what to do. So I could never let you have them.'

'That's all right,' Billy agreed. The warmth of the room, the steady ticking of a grandfather clock in the corner, and the sound and smell of whatever was bubbling away on the fire, made him feel sleepy. He yawned. 'I can't stay long,' he said, 'my sister is waiting outside in the lane. She'll wonder what's happened to me.'

'Not yet, boy,' the woman said. 'I don't even know your name.'

'It's Billy. Billy Parkin.'

'And where be you from, Billy Parkin?'

He yawned again. 'Just up the lane, in Railway Cottage,' he told her, wanting desperately to get out of here and back to Jess, away from the smell of the cooking pot, and the woman's strange eyes.

'I see.' She stared into space and Billy thought she had gone into a trance or something. Then she said, making him jump again, 'Well, Billy, don't you want to know what *my* name is?'

'I already know,' he said.

'It's Perizada,' she went on, as if she hadn't heard what he'd said. 'Born of the Fairies it means, and 'twas was my grandmother's name. She came to live here from Cornwall but I was born down there at St. Ives. My mother and father were Romany and we travelled all over the place in a horse-drawn caravan. Here, there and everywhere we went, until they died one soon after t'other and I had to come here and live with my grandma.' She drifted off again for a minute. 'Then,' she went on, 'my grandma died too and left me this cottage and 'tis where I've been ever since.'

'Why does everyone call you a witch, if you are Romany?' he asked.

Perizada laughed. 'Perizada the Mad Witch?' she said, smiling. 'Oh, I knows what them Gorgio's calls me behind my back don't you fret.' She gave the pot a stir then poked at the fire, sending a shower of sparks up the chimney. 'Tis because I make potions and lotions and things, and I can tell people their fortunes, if they want to know.' She gazed thoughtfully into the burning coals. 'I think that them folk, down in the village expect to see me ride about on a broomstick instead of a bike, though why they call me the mad witch, I don't rightly know. I'm a Romany and as sane as any of them. An' I don't do magic.' Her green eyes twinkled, and she gave Billy a wicked grin. 'Well, only when it suits me.'

'What's a Gorgio?' Billy asked.

''Tis someone who isn't Romany. *You're* a Gorgio, Billy.'

'Oh.' Billy looked up at the rows of bottles on the shelves. He pointed to one that was filled with mud-coloured liquid. 'What's in that bottle?' he asked.

'Ah,' she said, 'that be my special potion I sells to Doctor Bainbridge, who is a great believer in herb medicine and uses it for healing certain injuries and other ailments. Very efficacious it is, he tells me.'

'Efficacious? What does that mean?'

'It means 'tis good for you. That's what it means.'

He took a closer look at the bottle. 'It looks like the stuff he gave to me the other day when I hurt my back,' he said. 'It was horrible.'

'Made you better though, I'll bet,' Perizada said.

'Yes,' Billy agreed, remembering the awful, bitter taste of the brown liquid his mother had made him swallow three times a day for almost a week. He left his seat and moved over to the door. 'I really have to go now,' he said. 'My sister will be looking for me.'

'Will you come and see me again, Billy Parkin?' Perizada asked.

'I might.'

She stood up and towered above him. 'An' bring your little maid with you next time.'

Billy was puzzled. 'Maid?' he said. Only rich people had maids.

'Your sister, I mean.'

'I have two sisters; Jess and Shirley,' he said as she held open the door and he stepped out into the fresh air.

'What pretty names. Bring them both, if they want to come,' Perizada said, and without another word, closed the door in his face.

Billy could see Jess pacing up and down the lane. He hadn't been gone *that* long but she looked all red in the face and angry. 'What have you been doing?' she demanded, sounding just like their mother.

'Wouldn't you like to know,' he teased, winking at her.

'Well, are you going to tell me or not?'

'*Not.*' Billy lifted up the cart and, staring up at the sky, walked on, whistling to himself to make her even angrier. He loved tormenting her and seeing her face go all red and blotchy when she was annoyed with him.

'See if I care then,' she said, with a toss of her head. She wasn't going to let him see how much she was really *dying* to know all about Perizada the Mad Witch.

'She's a Romany woman, not a witch,' he said eventually, unable to keep it to himself any longer. 'And you're a *Gorgio*. I've promised to go and see her again … and take you with me.'

'I don't want to see her. And what's a Gorgio?'

'A person who's not a Romany, and I don't care if you want to see her or not,' he said as they continued their collecting from the remaining houses in Potters Lane. 'I want to find out more about her and *I'm* goin' back another day, so please yourself.'

The following day they spent taking the books to Danny's house, where they were sorted, the covers ripped off and the insides torn apart ready for the pulping machines. Billy was glad when Danny said they wouldn't have to take them to the village tomorrow after all because the farmer had offered to collect and deliver them in his lorry. It had been hard work pushing the cart up and down the lane, and his back hurt.

That night as he lay in bed, looking through the window at the moon, he thought about the woman, Perizada. No matter what anyone said, he would visit her again although he didn't care much for her spiteful black cats. Neither did he want, ever again to drink any of her terrible medicines, even if they *were* efficacious. He still wasn't sure whether she was a witch, a Romany or a bit of both. It didn't matter. She seemed very nice to him, and he wanted to find out more about her. As he drifted off to sleep. He wondered what she had done to make the villagers dislike her so much.

Chapter Nine

The German Airman

Because of one thing and another, Billy didn't make it back to Perizada's cottage the next day, or the day after that. Instead, he found himself caught up in the fear and excitement that gripped the village as he joined in the hunt for an armed and dangerous man on the loose.

At ten o'clock on the Saturday morning, the air raid siren on top of the fire station went off. Billy, who had gone to the Co-op to collect the week's rations for his mother, stopped on the brow of the hill leading down to the shop when he heard the whine of an aeroplane in trouble. He had long since learned to tell the difference between the sound of German and English aeroplanes. He looked up. 'That's a German Messerschmitt,' he shouted to someone passing by, 'and it's coming down.'

The aeroplane, engines screaming and smoke pouring from its tail, spun towards earth at great speed. Joined by a crowd of onlookers who had rushed from houses and shops, Billy watched as it just missed the church steeple, plunged to the ground and burst into flames. The explosion rocked the village, rattling windows and doors, and a pall of black smoke rose into the air.

Billy, enjoying all the excitement, spotted the parachutist. 'The pilot's baled out,' he said to the crowd. He pointed in the direction of some trees. 'Look, up there.' All eyes followed his finger to where a silver, pear-shaped object, carried along by the breeze, drifted slowly down towards the village. 'There's the parachute going down behind those trees over there, near the woods in Woodsmoke Lane. That's where I live.'

A man in the crowd scratched his head. 'Blimey,' he said, 'you're right. Better call out the Home Guard.' He looked at Billy and pointed downhill. 'See that row of cottages down there?'

'Yes, mister.'

'Knock on number three and ask for Harry Greentree. Tell 'im Albert Cooper sent you, and to muster his men together – there's a dangerous man on the loose who'll be armed and desperate.'

Billy ran as fast as his legs would carry him, hammered on the door of number three Victoria Terrace, and delivered the message to a tall, bespectacled man dressed in the uniform of the Home Guard. Harry Greentree squinted through his glasses. 'Did you see where the parachutist came down?' he asked.

Billy shook his head. 'No, mister. But it was somewhere over near to where I live in Woodsmoke Lane.'

'Ah.' Harry Greentree didn't seem too worried about this. He rubbed the bristles on his chin. 'Well, he's probably hangin' from some tree or other by now. An' I doubt if he's armed and desperate'. He collected his khaki overcoat from a peg in the hall and took a rifle from a cupboard under the stairs. 'I was just about to join my men in the bar of the Clipper and Bell,' he said, 'for our monthly meeting.

You run along home and don't worry about a thing. We'll have it all under control in no time.' Billy stood and watched as he marched off towards the village public house to pick up his men.

Word about the German pilot soon spread from one end of the village to the other. Mothers rounded up their children and, from behind closed windows and bolted doors, settled down to wait for something to happen.

When Billy reached home, he told his mother what Albert Cooper had said about the German being armed and desperate.

'The poor man's probably harmless, and scared to death,' she said.

Billy looked at her as if she'd gone mad. *'What?'*

'And take that look off your face. For all you know, he might have a mother back in Germany. Or even a wife and children who are all praying that he'll come home safely to them.'

'But he's a *German*,' Billy said. After all the terrible things the Germans had done, here was his mother standing up for one of them. 'They started the war.'

'Billy, the Germans don't want this war any more than we do but you're not old enough to understand such things.'

He looked daggers at her then stamped off into his bedroom. Red in the face with temper, he flung himself down on the bed. His own mother was a traitor – like one of those people he'd learned about at his old school back in Portsmouth, who took sides with the enemy. His Current Affairs teacher had told the class all about a man called William Joyce, known as Lord Haw Haw, who broadcast messages on the wireless, in which he told lies to frighten people. Billy remembered hearing his mother listening in to some of his programmes. He always sounded as if he had a cold. 'Germany calling, Germany calling,' he'd start with, and *she* always turned the wireless up so that she could hear the rest of what he was saying. Billy shot up on the bed, his thoughts all mixed up. Why was she interested in hearing what that man with the blocked up nose had to say? There was something funny about that. Was she really on the side of the Germans?

Shortly after darkness fell that evening, there was a tap on the front door. Billy's stomach turned over as he lifted a poker from the grate. His father hadn't come home from work yet, and Billy didn't know what to do. He looked at his mother and she went to the window to look out then nodded towards the door. He lifted the latch, opened it an inch and peered through the crack. It was one of the Home Guard, and he asked if there had been any strangers lurking about. Billy pulled the door back and shook his head.

'No, mister.'

'Have you heard about the German airman?'

'Yes, mister, I saw him come down this morning.'

The man shone a torch up and down the verandah as if expecting to find something. 'Well, be careful,' he said. 'Rumour has it that he's armed and desperate, though I doubt it. Harry Greentree reckons the poor bloke's probably hangin' from a tree somewhere, hoping to be rescued. Or,' he added, darkly, 'he might even be dead.'

'My dad'll be home any minute,' Billy said. He didn't like being stuck out here in the middle of nowhere with a dangerous man on the loose, and hoped his father hadn't had to work late. He shut the door and then went round the cottage making sure all the windows were closed.

'If any of you hear noises in the night,' his father said later, 'stay where you are and don't get up to see what it is. And that means you too Billy.'

By lunchtime the following day, despite the Home Guard combing the woods and fields around the village, there was still no sign of the German. Billy asked his mother if he and Jess could go out. He didn't want to stick around indoors all day, and besides, he wanted to look for the airman.

They set off to look behind the cottage where Danny lived. Here, the woods were denser and as they crept through the tangle of brambles, trying hard not to tread on any loose twigs, Billy thought about what their mother had said. He wondered what would happen if *he* found the airman. 'I don't see why we should be nice to him,' he said to Jess. 'He might have been the one who dropped the bombs that killed some of our friends.'

Jess agreed.

They had gone quite a long way into the woods when Jess caught her dress on a piece of rusty wire and couldn't move without it tearing. Billy said a swear word under his breath. Girls were always a nuisance, and he'd rather have searched for the German on his own.

'Stay still and keep quiet,' he said. As he struggled to unhook the wire, he thought he heard someone calling out for help. 'Shh,' he whispered as Jess opened her mouth to speak. He looked round and noticed something hanging from a clump of trees just ahead - a black-booted leg dangling loosely from one of the branches. His gaze travelled upwards, and he found himself staring at the terrified face of a young man dressed in the uniform of the German Luftwaffe. The straps on his parachute, with him still on the end of it, had caught in the branches of a tree, and one of his legs was trapped .

Billy grabbed Jess's arm to stop her as she made to dash off to find someone. First, he wanted to make up his mind what to do. Should he let her go and get help to release the German? Or leave him hanging in the trees to teach him a lesson? The Home Guard would find him anyway. But what if, by the time they did, he had died? Perhaps mum's right, he thought, and there *is* a family back in Germany, who want him home with them. He stood and watched the man with interest for a while. Then he let go of Jess and told her to stay where she was while he went to get help.

When he reached Railway Cottage, he saw his father leaning over the gate looking for him and Jess.

Billy could tell that he was angry that their mother had allowed them out instead of making them stay in the safety of their own home. 'We've found the airman,' he said with a wide grin. 'He's stuck up a tree.'

'Where's Jess?'

'I left her watching him.'

He thought his father would explode. 'You're a stupid little idiot. What did you want to do a thing like that for? Get down the shed and look for something we can use to defend ourselves if we have to, and I'll go and find her.'

Billy dashed off down the side of the cottage to the shed. From a selection of tools, he chose a penknife in case he might need it to cut the parachute cords, and a wooden mallet in case the airman became violent. He then ran back through the woods to where he'd left Jess, and found his father trying to make conversation with the German, who was still stuck between the branches of the tree. Billy wondered how they were going to be able to release him.

'You're good at climbing,' his father said. 'See if you can get up high enough to untangle the parachute.' He pointed to the penknife. 'Use that to cut the cords if you have to,' he said, nodding towards the top of the tree, 'but watch out for him up there.' He helped Billy onto one of the lower branches and watched as he shinned up the tree like a monkey.

When Billy drew level with the German, the two of them eyed each other suspiciously. Billy showed him the penknife, being careful to keep it well out of reach, and made signs that he was only going to use it to cut him free. Settling himself on a sturdy branch, he leaned against it and began sawing at the parachute cords.

'What's your name, mister,' he said.

'Ernst Hartmann.'

'Ernst?'

The German nodded.

'I'm called Billy Parkin.' He noticed the German was keeping a wary eye on the penknife.

'Grab hold of that branch,' he said, hoping the German would understand. 'In case you fall or somethin'. Why were you flying over here?'

'I vas lost.'

Billy's father, who had been watching from below, called out to be careful. He didn't want Billy or the German falling out of the tree, he said.

'We need a ladder, Dad,' Billy called out.

'I'll go and get one, but be careful, Billy.'

Once the remains of the parachute were untangled and Ernst, who offered up no resistance, was free and able to climb down to the ground, Billy's father frisked him for arms. He found nothing, and decided to take him back to Railway Cottage and await the arrival of the Home Guard. Jess had already been sent ahead to warn their mother, and Billy despatched to the village to look for Harry Greentree and his men.

When Billy came back, he found the Ernst Hartmann tucking into a plate of sandwiches. He started to ask his mother why an enemy should be eating *their* rations when there was barely enough to go round as it was. She silenced him with a look, daring him to say anything.

When Ernst had finished eating, she asked him if he had a wife back home.

'Ja,' Ernst replied. 'Frau Berta Hartmann.'

'Do you have any children?'

'Nein.'

'Nine?' Billy put in.

'Nein in German means none,' his mother said.

'Where do you live in Germany?' Billy asked,.

Ernst's face darkened angrily and his eyes turned cold. 'I live in what is left of Cologne,' he said. 'You English haf bombed my beautiful city.' He brought his fist down on the table and the cups and saucers rattled. 'But when we haf won the war,' he went on, in broken English, ''ve vill rebuild all that you haf destroyed, and the Deutschland vill be as great as it vas before.'

Billy knew that, just like Portsmouth, Cologne had been bombed until there was nothing much left of it except for piles of rubble. He could hardly believe it when he heard his father apologising, and wondered what his parents were thinking of to treat an enemy as if he were an old friend. This German, sitting here as if he owned the place, had probably helped destroy Portsmouth, *and* all the other places that had been bombed in England. *And*, Billy thought to himself, I bet if it were one of our own airmen, no German family would give him food and shelter. If they did, they'd be shot.

Half an hour later, to everyone's relief, six men of the Home Guard, accompanied by two policemen arrived. 'Two of you would have been enough,' Billy's father said. He pointed to their rifles. 'And you won't need those, either.'

Harry Greentree, who was in charge, shook his head. 'Don't be fooled by the blue eyes and fair hair,' he said. 'Given half a chance, he'd do something desperate to get away if he could.'

As they escorted Ernst from the cottage, Billy heard his mother asking the men to be nice to their prisoner. 'Don't worry, missus,' Harry Greentree said. 'I've a son myself ... in the Air Force as it happens.'

They reached the gate and Ernst turned round and waved to the Parkins. Then, to everyone except Harry Greentree's surprise, for he wasn't easily fooled, he drew himself up to attention, clicked his heels smartly together and before anyone could stop him, raised one arm in a Nazi salute. 'Heil Hitler!' he shouted, then, with his head in the air he marched away, limping slightly, down the lane between his escorts.

'What will they do to him?' Billy wanted to know. When his mother said that the British would treat him well, and he might even get to work on a local farm, he felt angry again. 'They ought to shoot him,' he said, remembering Dave Spiller. 'They ought to shoot *all* Germans.'

Chapter Ten

Where is Dad?

'I'm sitting next to George Bunn,' Billy said at the end of his first day at Cowplain school. 'An' he keeps kicking me under the desk.'

'Well, kick him back, then,' Jess said.

'I did, an' he told Miss Harry, the Geography teacher, an' she told *me* off.'

'*That's* not fair.'

Billy finished off his tea. 'No, it's not,' he said, 'but I'm goin' to get him back after school one day. You wait and see. What's *your* school like?'

'It's all right,' Jess replied, 'but I'll be glad when I go to Cowplain in September. And Shirley started blubbing when mum told her she'd have to go to school next week.'

'Aw, she's always blubbin' about somethin' or other.' Billy left the table and went out into the garden to find his mother to ask if he could go out.

'Not yet,' she said. 'I've something to tell you all first.' They went back inside where she told them her news. 'The café up on the main road want someone to wait on tables and help in the kitchen. I've seen the owners and they've offered me the job. Now that there are two lots of rent to find, the extra money will come in useful.'

Billy couldn't believe it. Mothers didn't go out to work. They stayed at home, looked after the house and did the cooking and the washing. 'What about us?' he said, thinking about how empty his stomach always felt when he got home from school. He couldn't imagine what it would be like to get home, tired and hungry, to an empty house with no tea ready. 'Who's goin' to get our tea?'

'I'll be working while you're at school,' she said, 'and I don't think any of you will starve if your tea isn't on the table the minute you get home.'

Billy didn't want to come home from school and find Jess taking charge and bossing everyone about. Although, he supposed, it might mean he could have some pocket money like most other boys his age. 'When do you have to start?' he said.

'Next Monday.'

'But that's washing day.'

'Try your best not to be stupid, Billy,' his mother said. 'I'm doing this to help your dad with the rent. And right from this minute you can all start getting used to doing more to help around the house. You, Jess can put some water on to boil and wash the dishes. Shirley will wipe them and put them away.' She turned to Billy. 'And as for you –the verandah's covered in leaves and needs sweeping. So get on with it - *now*.'

Without another word, she marched out into the garden leaving them staring after her as if she'd gone mad. This was not like their mother. Something was wrong.

Billy broke the silence. 'Suppose we'd better do as she says,' he grumbled. He fetched a broom from the kitchen, Jess put the kettle on and sprinkled some soap flakes into the sink, and Shirley looked around for a tea towel.

'Is there something wrong with mum? Jess said. Having finished their tasks, they were sitting around the fire waiting for their mother to come in from the garden, each wondering what had happened to put her in such a bad mood.

'I don't know,' Billy said. 'She's acting all funny.'

Shirley looked up from the book she was reading. 'Is she going to die?'

Billy gave her a dark look. 'Don't be silly,' he said. 'Of course she's not going to die. I expect she's just fed up with the war and is missing Portsmouth. That's all.'

'Well,' Shirley replied, '*I'm* fed up and want to go back to Portsmouth too. I *hate* it here.'

Billy left his chair and went over to the window. He looked across the lane at the woods, where the trees were just breaking into leaf. Even though in the beginning, he hadn't wanted to move, he now loved living here, where everything was so peaceful and quiet, and couldn't understand how anyone would want to go back to live among the ruins of a dusty old town. 'You're *stupid,* ' he said to Shirley.

Outside in the orchard, their mother sat on a wooden bench wondering how she was going to tell them that their dad hadn't come home last night and that she had no idea what had become of him. The B.B.C news on the wireless at lunchtime had reported a "heavy and sustained attack by German bombers last night on the south coast, the worst of the raids centred on the dockyard area of Portsmouth. There are a number of casualties." He was probably helping with the rescue operations but on the other hand, he could be one of the casualties himself. The thought sent shivers down her spine and she rose quickly from her seat and went indoors.

'I'm afraid your dad didn't come home last night,' she said. 'And I don't know how I can find out what's happened to him.'

So, that was it. Billy felt sick. A cold, empty feeling crept over him and he shivered. He couldn't imagine what it would be like not to have his dad around. 'There was an air raid last night,' he said. 'I could hear it going on.'

'Yes, I know,' she replied, 'I heard it too. And I listened to the news this morning. Portsmouth has been badly hit, especially around the dockyard.'

Billy jumped to his feet. 'I'll go down to the village,' he said, 'and ask them in the Clipper and Bell if they would telephone the police to try and find out what has happened.'

'I'll come with you,' Jess offered.

'And me,' Shirley said.

'No, you stay here with mum, Shirley.' Billy didn't want *her* having a screaming fit if the air raid siren went off while they were out.

'You won't be allowed in the Clipper and Bell,' his mother said. 'You're not old enough.'

Billy refused to listen. 'We'll knock on Harry Greentree's door then,' he said, 'and ask him to do it for us.'

'Well, just be careful. It'll soon be getting dark.'

'We will,' Billy promised. 'And don't worry, Mum. Dad will be all right. You'll see.'

Harry Greentree remembered the Parkins and how they had helped capture the German pilot. 'I'll just nip across to the pub and see what I can find out.' He said. 'You two sit here on this wall and wait. I won't be long.'

As they waited for Harry Greentree, Jess asked Billy if he thought their dad was dead.

'No, I don't.'

'Why don't you?'

Billy didn't know why he thought their father was still alive. He just had this *feeling* about it. 'Because he's our dad,' he replied. 'That's why.'

'Dorothy McEnzie's dad died the other day,' Jess said.

'Who's Dorothy McEnzie?'

'She's a girl in my class at school.'

Billy didn't really want to know about this girl's dad, especially if it was something horrible, but he asked anyway. 'What happened to him?' he said.

Jess shrugged. 'I don't know. He was a fireman. He went to work in Portsmouth one day, there was an air raid and he didn't ever come back.'

Billy felt more worried than he wanted to admit. 'Shut up, *you*,' he said, 'I don't want to listen to any more. Our dad's all right. I know he is.'

A grim-faced Harry Greentree came back with bad news. 'All telephone lines are down,' he said. 'I'm sorry but there's nothing anyone can do to find out what's happened to your dad.'

'Thanks, Mr Greentree,' Billy said and he and Jess set off for home. They had almost reached Catherton Lane when they saw two policemen walking towards them. When they drew level, Billy stopped. 'Excuse me, sir,' he said, 'could you help us?'

'What seems to be the trouble, son?' one of them, a large man with three stripes on his sleeves, asked.

'Our dad works in the dockyard in Pompey, 'Billy explained, 'and he didn't come home last night. Our mum's goin' mad with worry. She says there was a big raid over Pompey and she doesn't know what has happened to our dad.'

The sergeant shook his head. 'Aye, that there was,' he said. 'A lot of dads didn't get home last night. It's Bedlam down there and no one knows what's what.' He turned to his younger colleague. 'Isn't that right, constable?'

'Yes, sergeant, that's right.'

'Don't' even know how many casualties there are yet, do they, constable?'

'No, sergeant.'

'Well, thank you anyway,' Billy said. 'But I 'spect our dad'll turn up.'

71

'That's the spirit, son.' The sergeant produced a notebook from his breast pocket. 'Tell you what', he said, licking the end of a lead pencil, 'give me your name and address and if we hear anything, we'll call round and let you know.'

When Billy and Jess arrived home, their mother was still sitting in their father's armchair. Shirley was missing and the fire had gone out.

'Where's old moaning Minnie ?' Billy said.

'If you mean your sister, Shirley, she's gone next door to look at the kittens,' she replied. 'Were you able to find out anything?'

Billy shook his head and told her about the telephone lines being down. 'But we met two policemen and gave them our address. They've promised to call round if they have any news.' He switched the wireless on just in time for the latest news bulletin.

'This is the BBC Home Service. Here is the news and this is Alvar Liddell reading it. The South Coast suffered heavy damage and many casualties in last night's bombing raids. Badly hit was Portsmouth dockyard, and rescuers are still trying to reach a number of workers trapped beneath the rubble. Latest reports state that so far, twenty people have lost their lives, with many more injured. Relatives are being informed as and when information becomes available.'

The clear, precise tones of the announcer faded as Billy turned the volume down.

'That's what they said this morning,' his mother said.

At seven o'clock, Shirley went to bed, having announced that the kitten her mother had said she could have would be ready to leave its mother at the weekend, and she would like to call it Raffles.

'Call it what you like,' Billy said without interest. At nine o'clock, he and Jess went to bed. I'll never be able to sleep, he thought, as he climbed into bed, his mind turning over and over. What would happen to them all if their dad never came home again? They would have to go back to Portsmouth for a start, but that wasn't the worst of it. There wouldn't be any money to live on, and they'd starve. Then their mother would die and he would have to look after Jess and Shirley. Worse still, they might all have to go into a home. Be separated and never see each other again. He didn't like his sisters much but they were better than no family at all. By midnight, he had tossed and turned so much that all the blankets were on the floor and he was freezing. He re-made the bed and climbed back in but still couldn't get off to sleep.

Sometime later, he heard a sharp rap at the front door. He crept out of bed, opened his bedroom door a few inches and stood in the shadows to watch. He saw his mother pull down the window and peer out into the darkness. Then she unbolted the front door to let the two policemen he'd met earlier step inside.

'We met your two nippers earlier on,' the sergeant explained, 'and we took your name and address in case there was any news.'

'And is there?'

The constable consulted his notebook. 'Your husband is Alfred James Parkin, known as Fred?'

Billy's heart was in his mouth. It sounded serious. His saw his mother nod.

'Well, he's safe, Mrs Parkin. We managed to contact the dockyard police and they have confirmed that he has been helping with the rescue operations. Trouble is,' he went on, snapping his notebook shut, 'there's no transport to bring him home tonight so he's volunteered to stay and give what help he can. He'll be home sometime tomorrow.'

Billy watched her let the two policemen out into the night and when she sat in the armchair and started crying, he went to see what was wrong. 'What's the matter, Mum?' he said. His father was safe, the policeman had said so. So why was she upset?

'Oh, Billy, I'm so relieved and happy,' she said, wiping her eyes in her pinafore. 'I really thought your dad might have been killed in that air raid.'

'Aw, Mum, I *told* you he'd be all right, didn't I?'

'Yes, Billy, you did.' She left the chair and went out to the kitchen. 'Now, would you like a cup of cocoa?'

Billy scratched his head. Fancy crying when you're happy. He'd never understand grown ups and their funny ways. 'Yes, please,' he said.

Chapter Eleven

The Fight

It was after the Whitsun holiday that George Bunn began tormenting Billy. On the first day back at school, Billy, whose favourite subject was English, opened a brand new exercise book and settled down to write a composition about how the working classes lived in Victorian times. The class had recently covered the topic during history lessons, and Billy found it interesting. He had almost filled a page when a blob of black ink landed right in the middle and spread itself outwards, forming a large blot. He looked sideways at George, who was staring at the ceiling and whistling quietly between his teeth.

'I'll get you for that later, Bunn,' Billy threatened. 'Just you wait and see.' He saw the English master, Horace Skinter, raise his head and fix him with a dark look from his sharp little eyes.

'Be quiet, Parkin!' Horace Skinter ordered, 'unless you wish to take a walk to the headmaster's office.'

'Sorry, sir.' Billy turned to a fresh page in his book and began his essay again. He would get his own back on George Bunn later.

His chance came later that morning when he found himself behind George in the dinner queue and watched him feeding greedy eyes on his plate of steaming vegetable stew. Billy pretended to stumble, and fell heavily against him. The plate shot out of George's hands and fell with a crash to the floor, half of its contents spilling down the front of his shirt, the rest spreading in a gooey mess under the counter.

Billy laughed behind his hands as the History teacher, Miss Thorncroft, who had been supervising, flew into a rage. 'You stupid boy, George Bunn,' she yelled. 'Go out into the kitchen and ask for a bucket and mop – with which *you* can clear up the mess you've made.'

By the time George had finished mopping up the puddle on the floor, there was very little stew left for him. 'Serves you right,' the dinner lady said as she scraped the bottom of the tin and slopped the contents onto a clean plate. 'Should look what you're doing.'

This brought the feud between him and Billy to a head.

'Me and my pals will get you after school,' George warned as they returned to afternoon classes. 'You'll be sorry for what you did.'

Billy couldn't remember having ever seen George, who always seemed to be on his own, with any friends. 'Oh yeah,' he replied. 'You and who's army?'

'You'll see,' George threatened.

At four o'clock, when school finished, Billy sauntered to the gates to find George, in the company of two other boys Billy didn't know, waiting for him. One of them, a rough-looking character, planted himself in front of Billy and refused to let him pass.

'You did our friend out of his dinner,' he said. 'An' we don't like our friend goin' hungry, do we, Mike?

The boy called Mike shook his head. 'That's right, Frank,' he agreed. 'An' we don't like 'vacuees, either.'

'What you got to say about that then, Pompey Fleabag?' the one called Frank asked, pushing his face into Billy's.

Billy sniffed and wiped his nose in his shirtsleeve. 'He asked for it,' he said, flinching as the one called Mike squeezed his arm in a vice-like grip to stop him running away. 'He messed up my English.'

'Ah, shame,' Mike said.

'Yeah. *Shame*,' Frank agreed.

Billy tried to wriggle free. 'Let me go,' he shouted, attracting the attention of a crowd of schoolchildren who were hanging around, hoping to see a good fight. 'Leave me alone.' Once again, the face of Brendan Trapper appeared before his eyes. Would the ghost of the bully who had made his life such a misery, before meeting a sudden death in an air raid, haunt him forever?

'C'mon, then,' George said, hopping from foot to foot, fists clenched into balls.

Billy removed his coat and placed it, with his gas mask, on the ground. George stopped prancing around and did likewise. They both raised their fists.

What started out as an ordinary scrap between the two boys would have finished without much harm done to either, but what George said next made

Billy lose his temper. 'Your dad's a coward,' he yelled. 'Why aint he in the Navy like my dad?'

'He's too old,' Billy shouted back. 'He was in the last war, and he isn't a coward, either.'

'He's yellow. That's what he is!'

'He is *not*!' Billy could feel his temper rising. 'He nearly died a few weeks ago, rescuing people from burning buildings in the dockyard. So put that in your pipe and smoke it.'

'Billy Parkin's dad's a coward,' George shouted to anyone who was listening.

Billy clenched his fist and brought it up with a smack under George's chin. Then he hit him again, only harder. No one called *his* dad a coward and got away with it.

George fell to the ground and lay motionless.

'What've you done?' George's "friends" weren't really friends at all. They had only agreed to back him up in exchange for a catapult and half his sweet ration, and didn't really want to get involved in the fight themselves. Mike pointed to the prone body lying on the ground. 'You've knocked him out.'

'*Killed* `im,' the other boy said, darkly.

Billy didn't know exactly what he had done to George, and now he could see Horace Skinter making his way across the school playground. Skinter didn't like what he called "outsiders" like Billy who didn't belong, and Billy knew there would be trouble.

'You've knocked him out cold,' Skinter said, kneeling down beside the victim. Billy could see George's eyeballs moving under his lids. He watched as, slowly and with great drama, George opened his eyes and squinted at the concerned face of the master hovering over him. Apart from a lump swelling up on his chin, he seemed all right and Skinter told him to get to his feet.

'I will *not*,' Skinter yelled, 'have boys fighting in the school grounds.' He jabbed a finger into Billy's chest. 'You, Parkin, will report to the headmaster's office at nine-fifteen sharp tomorrow morning.' He turned his attention to George, and his voice had a kindlier tone. 'Are you all right, Bunn?' he asked.

'Yes thank you, sir,' George replied with a weak smile, giving Billy a furtive sidelong glance. 'I don't know why Parkin attacked me. I aint done nothin' to 'im.'

'*Haven't done anything to him*, Bunn,' Skinter corrected as he turned to go back into school, muttering to himself about what a waste of time it was, trying to teach these boys proper English.

By the time Billy had walked to the top of the road, with George Bunn keeping a good ten yards' behind, the bus had already left. He decided not to wait for the next one but to walk the two miles home. He'd covered about a quarter of a mile when he realised George was still ambling along behind. Billy stopped.

'What do *you* want?' he said, as George caught up with him.

'I didn't mean to get you into trouble with old Skinter,' George said.

'Well, you should learn to keep your big mouth shut, George Bunn.'

George's face was bright red and there were dark smudges under his eyes where he'd been crying. A purple bruise had spread itself across the swelling on his chin. 'How did *I* know Skinter would turn up?' he said.

Billy began to feel a bit sorry for him. It couldn't be very nice if your dad was away and you didn't even know whether he was alive or dead. All the same, because of George Bunn, he was going to have to face the headmaster tomorrow morning. And that could mean only one thing – the cane. 'Shove off,' he said, as they turned into Woodsmoke Lane.

George shuffled up the path to his caravan. 'I hate you, Parkin,' he called over his shoulder. 'An' I hope ole' Armitage gives you ten strokes tomorrow.'

The following morning, at exactly nine-fifteen, Billy presented himself at the headmaster's office. Skinter stood with his back to the window, looking pleased with himself.

'Explain yourself, Parkin,' headmaster James Armitage said. He was a kindly man who understood the problems evacuees faced trying to fit in to a community of people who didn't want them. He also knew that George Bunn was something of a misfit, and that Horace Skinter thought that anyone who hadn't lived in Horndean since they were born had no business to live there.

Billy related the previous day's events, and James Armitage listened.

'Well,' he said eventually, 'I don't intend to punish you too severely this time, but I will not tolerate fighting on school premises.' He stood up and crossed the room to where he kept his cane. 'Two strokes,' he said, brandishing the weapon in the air as if it were a sword. 'Which hand do you write with, Parkin?'

'This one, sir,' Billy said, holding up his right hand.'

'Then show me the left one.'

Billy held out his left hand and gritted his teeth together. He'd never had the cane before and didn't know what to expect. It came down with a swish twice, hard on his hand, and he felt tears welling up in his eyes. He could see Skinter smirking to himself, and swallowed hard. He wasn't going to give the English teacher the satisfaction of seeing him cry, even though the palm of his hand felt as if the skin had been ripped off.

'Off you go, back to your lessons,' James Armitage said.

'Yes, sir.' Billy scuttled away, rubbing his hand on the side of his trousers. He went back to his class and slipped into his seat next to George.

'Did it hurt?' George whispered, spraying spittle into Billy's ear.

'Did what hurt?'

'Ole' Armitage's cane.'

Billy forced a smile. 'Nope,' he said. 'I didn't get it.'

'Liar,' George said, giving him a sideways kick under the desk.

Chapter Twelve

Another Meeting

Billy fished in his trouser pocket, took out a note that Meg had passed to him on the bus and read it. It was from Danny to say that there would be a meeting of the Woodlarks on the first Saturday in July to arrange a garden fete in aid of Mrs Churchill's Aid to Russia Fund.

"Please come if you and Jess can as there are lots of things to sort out," he'd written. *"Ten o'clock, in the usual place."*

When Billy and Jess arrived, they found Meg already there with a boy and girl they had never seen before. 'This is Nancy Betts and her brother, Sam.' Danny said. 'They live in The Avenue and their dad says we can hold the fete in their front garden as long as we clear up afterwards.'

They all settled down on the grass, and Danny handed round pencils and paper.

'I thought,' Danny said, 'that we'd have a few stalls, some games like Hoopla, and Skittles and a raffle, but all ideas will be welcome.'

'Why don't we have a fortune teller?' Billy said. 'Someone's mum could dress up as a gipsy or something and read palms, or maybe teacups.'

'That's a good idea,' Danny agreed.

'We could use the old gipsy caravan in our garden, 'Sam offered. 'We'd have to ask our mum and dad but I don't suppose they'd mind.'

Billy thought quickly. 'I know just the person,' he said. 'A lady I met the other day, called Perizada.'

'The Mad Witch?' Meg said.

'She's *not* mad, and she isn't a witch, either. She's a Romany woman.'

'How do *you* know so much about her?' Danny asked.

'I called there when we were collecting books.'

'I thought we told you not to.'

'I don't have to do what you tell me,' Billy said, angrily. 'It's none of your business who I see. And if you don't like it, you can take my name off the club. And Jess's too.' He turned to the others. 'Who wants the *Romany Lady* to read fortunes at the fete?'

They all did, except Danny, because they wanted to see the strange woman their mothers talked about in whispers.

'I'll go round and ask her,' Billy said.

'Anyone have any other ideas?' Danny asked, changing the subject.

'My dad has some flags in the shed,' Meg said. 'They're left over from the coronation of the King and Queen. I think he'd let us borrow them and we could hang them from the trees in Nancy's garden.'

Danny made a note of this. 'Good idea,' he said. 'And if anyone else has any suggestions, please let me know.' He turned to Sam and Nancy. 'You won't forget to ask your parents about the caravan, will you?'

Everyone agreed to hold the fete on the first Saturday in August. 'Are we going to meet once a week?' Billy asked, 'to get things ready' He didn't see any reason why Danny should have all the say in this. It was everyone's fete, not just his.

'I was coming to that in a minute,' Danny replied. 'We'll meet here on Saturday mornings at ten. All right? And could you ask your dad, Meg, to paint some posters to put in the shop windows?'

'Yes,' Meg said, and the meeting closed.

When Billy and Jess reached home, they saw their mother talking over the garden fence to Meg's mother. 'Go indoors,' she said.' 'I've something to tell you. I won't be a minute.'

'Somethin's the matter,' Billy whispered to Jess as they went in through the back door and waited. 'Mum looks really upset.'

'Shh. Here she comes.'

'George Bunn's mother has had a telegram to say that his dad's been killed at sea,' their mother told them. 'Meg's mother heard the news when she was in the Co-op collecting her rations. Poor Mrs Bunn, and George. I'll go and see them, to say how sorry we are.' She looked at Billy. 'And you can come with me.'

Billy didn't want to go. He and George Bunn were still enemies and he hadn't forgiven him for getting him into trouble at school. All the same, he felt sorry that George's dad was now lying at the bottom of the sea somewhere, and would never come home again.

A red-eyed Mrs Bunn let them into the tiny caravan. George, his gaze fixed on the wall opposite on which hung a photograph of a young man in naval uniform, ignored the visitors. Billy stood in the doorway not knowing what to say. Why had his mother made him come here? She should have come on her own, not dragged him along. He was only twelve and didn't know how to talk to someone who'd just lost their dad. George turned to look at him, a scowl on his face.

'Sorry about your dad,' Billy said.

'Why don't you push off?' George turned away and went back to staring at the photograph.

Billy clenched his fists into balls. He wanted to punch George Bunn, hard. 'I only said I'm sorry.'

'Liar,' George said. 'You don't care. You've still got your dad and you aint sorry at all.'

Chapter Thirteen

The Fortune Teller

The following Wednesday after school, Billy decided to go and see Perizada, and he asked Jess if she wanted to go with him. 'Please yourself. I don't care if you come or not,' he said when she pulled a face.

'All right, I'll come, but I don't think she ought to read fortunes at our fete. No one likes her and what will they say?'

'Who cares what anyone says?' Billy said. 'And you're beginning to sound like Danny Palmer with his posh talk an' big ideas.'

'Where are you two going?' their mother asked as they were leaving the cottage.

Billy gave Jess a warning look to stop her saying anything. 'Just down Potters Lane,' he said, 'to see someone about the fete.' If she knew they were going to see Perizada, she'd put a stop to it.

'All right, but don't be long. Shirley's not well and wants someone to sit with her.'

Billy pulled a face. Shirley was only after a bit of attention and *he* wasn't going to sit reading stupid fairy stories to her.

Perizada's cats arched their backs and spat at Billy and Jess. 'They won't hurt you,' he said, feeling much braver than the last time he was here. He reached up and tapped on the black, iron knocker.

'Ah, come in,' Perizada said as she opened the door. She was dressed differently this time, in a short green frock that changed colour every time she moved. 'I see you've brought one of your little maids with you. And what be *your* name?' she asked, her cold, green eyes fixed on Jess's terrified face. 'Don't be afraid, my maid. I won't be doing you no harm – no matter what folks round and about here say about me.'

'Jess.'

'Well Jess, sit you down – and you too Billy.' She gave a funny little laugh. 'See, boy I've remembered your name.'

They sat side by side on a long wooden settle under the window and Billy noticed the cauldron still bubbling away as before, although this time, there was a different smell about the place. A sweet, flowery scent that was rather pleasant.

'Flower water,' Perizada said, before he could ask. 'You shall have some, if you like, Jess. Now, how would you like a drink?' She fetched two glasses from a shelf and filled them with an amber coloured liquid. 'Try this,' she said. ''Tis made from cowslips I picked myself over in the woods. Go on, t'won't do you no harm.'

It was cool and sweet and tasted a little bit like honey. Billy didn't like it much but Jess loved the unusual taste and sipped at hers while he held his breath and swallowed it quickly. He was getting a bit worried about the time. 'We've come to ask you a favour Perizada,' he said at last.

'And what be that, boy?'

'We're havin' a garden fete in August in aid of Mrs Churchill's Aid to Russia Fund and wondered if you would come and tell fortunes?'

Perizada's face darkened. 'I don't think so,' she said. 'People down in the village don't like me and, except for those whose fortunes I've already told, they won't want me spelling out the future to them.'

'*Please.*' He'd look really silly if she wouldn't do it, and Danny would enjoy that. He fidgeted about while she thought it over.

'Well, maybe,' she said presently. 'You come back tomorrow and I'll tell you yes or no. And I'll find your little maid a bottle of my flower water to make her smell nice.'

'We'll have to go now,' Billy said. 'Our mum will have dinner ready.'

'Will you be coming back tomorrow, then?' Perizada asked.

'Yes,' Billy said. 'After school.'

'Well, what do you think of her?' he asked Jess as they walked back up the lane.

'She does look a bit like a witch,' Jess said, 'but she's quite nice.'

'I told you so.'

The next afternoon, they returned to Perizada's cottage and Billy told her that there might be a real gipsy caravan for her to use if she would come. She said she would if she could have a large table for the cards.

'Don't you use one of those crystals balls?' he said, feeling just a bit disappointed at the thought of Perizada telling fortunes with a pack of playing cards, like those his father used to play Patience.

'I do sometimes,' Perizada said. 'But folk seem to believe in the Tarot cards more'n the ball. And they're not like ordinary playing cards.'

'Tarot?'

Perizada took a pack of cards from a nook at the side of the fireplace and offered them to Billy. 'Have a look,' she said.

He examined them. 'What do all the pictures mean?' he asked. 'And you told me you couldn't read.'

Perizada shook her head. 'It's best you don't know,' she said quietly. 'The secret of the Tarot is known to only a few and should be left like that. And I can't read, but my grandmother taught me how to use the cards.'

'Oh. Well, how much do you think we should charge for a reading?' Billy asked.

'I think one shilling.'

'No. One shilling and thruppence.'

'All right then.' Perizada said. 'One shilling and three-pence it is.'

Billy noticed Jess staring at Perizada in a strange way as the gipsy went to a cupboard in the corner of the room and took out a bottle of flower water.

'Just a small drop here and there,' she said, handing it to Jess. 'It'll make you feel nice.'

Jess took the bottle and then gave it back. 'I want to go home now, 'she said. 'I don't think my mum would like me putting scent on.'

Perizada looked down her long, thin nose. 'And what have I done to upset you, my little maid?' she said, her strange green eyes riveted on Jess's face.

'I don't feel very well.'

'Well, you were all right five minutes' ago, child,' she said, 'but if you want to go, then I won't try and stop you.'

Billy was as mad as a hornet and, as he and Jess walked home, he went off at her for upsetting his new friend. 'She might not want to do the fortune telling 'cos of *you*,' he bawled at her as she stormed off up the lane.

'She's horrible,' Jess shouted back.

'She's *not*!'

'She is *too*. And the others are right. She *is* a witch.'

Billy, in a temper, caught a stone in the toe of his boot and kicked it up the lane. 'Well don't think I'm taking you there ever again,' he said. 'You were rude to her.'

'*Good,*' Jess shouted back. 'I don't ever want to see her again anyway.'

'Goodness gracious me, whenever I see you, there is always a lot of noise going on.' They both swung round to see Mrs Lavender Baggit hanging over her garden gate. 'What's all the fuss about this time? And were my eyes deceiving me or did I just see you come from Crows Nest Cottage?'

Jess kept quiet but Billy was still in a temper. 'Yes, we have,' he shouted. 'We've just come from Crows Nest Cottage where we've been visiting *a very good friend.*'

This left Mrs Lavender Baggit speechless for a few seconds. 'Well,' she said, when she had recovered, 'I'm not too sure your mother would approve of you visiting such a person. And I think she should be told.'

'She already knows,' he lied.

Mrs Baggit lifted her enormous bosom from where it had been resting on the top of the gate, and turned to go indoors. 'I hope you are telling the truth,' she said, as she waddled along the path towards her front door.

'I am,' Billy called after her, and he and Jess laughed, their argument forgotten for the time being.

'We'll have to tell mum, now that old biddy knows,' Billy said as they turned into the gate of Railway Cottage.

Their mother wasn't pleased. 'I've heard all sorts of things about that woman,' she said. 'And you are not to go there again. Is that clear?'

'Aw, Mum,' Billy said, as they sat down to their dinner. 'We've asked her to tell fortunes at the fete, and she's said she will.'

'Then you will have to tell her you've changed your mind. And stop talking with your mouth full of food.'

They ate the rest of the meal in silence, with Billy wondering what he was going to do about Perizada. If only that old nosy parker hadn't seen them, no-one would have found out until it was too late. Later that evening, when he was supposed to be in bed, he stood at his bedroom door and listened to his mother telling his father that she'd forbidden them to go there again.

'If you do that, Doris,' he heard his father say, 'you'll be lowering yourself to the level of the villagers who seem to be conducting some sort of hate campaign against the woman.'

'So you think it's all right for them to visit her, Fred?'

'You don't want to listen to every bit of gossip you hear,' he said. 'And I don't see any harm in them visiting her as long as they tell you where they're going, do you?'

'I suppose not.'

Billy crept back to bed and immediately fell asleep.

Chapter Fourteen

The Fete

During the week before the fete, Billy called on Perizada to make sure she would still be going, and Jess and Shirley knocked on doors for things to sell on the bric-a-brac stall. Their mother filled some paper bags with fruit from the orchard. 'Charge sixpence a bag,' she told Billy. 'Don't sell for less.'

The day dawned dry, warm and sunny and at seven o'clock in the morning, everyone assembled at Sam and Nancy's house to set up in time for the ten o'clock opening. Billy helped Sam and Nancy string the red, white and blue flags over the gate and through the trees. Nancy's dad had painted a board which read 'LET PERIDAZA TELL YOUR FORTUNE FOR ONLY ONE & THRUPPENCE, and they propped it up against one of the shafts of the caravan, which stood, resplendent in all its gaudy colours, in a corner beneath a Sycamore tree.

As usual, Danny took charge of everything. 'You can go around selling draw tickets,' he said to Billy. The prize is a bag of sugar. Jess and Meg will do the White Elephant stall, and your mother and Shirley, the Guess the number of Buttons competition. The winner gets a pot of jam. Sam and Nancy have said they'll serve up refreshments, and look after the Skittles.'

'What about *you*?' Billy asked. 'Or are you just going to stand around bossing everyone else about?'

'No need to be funny,' Danny said. 'I'm going to do the Hoopla.'

By five minutes to ten, everything was ready for the opening by Danny's older brother Tim who was home on leave from the R.A.F. He looked very handsome in his Pilot Officer's uniform and Jess immediately fell in love with him. 'Wish I was old enough to be his girl-friend,' she whispered to Meg.

'Don't be so daft,' Meg replied. 'He's probably got one already.'

Mrs Lavender Baggit, wearing a dreadful, flowered frock and a wide-brimmed straw hat covered in artificial cherries, was the first to arrive. She looked, Billy thought, like a windblown flower garden. 'Where's this fortune-teller then?' she demanded to know, just as Perizada, at five past ten, pushed her bicycle through the gate.

'Sorry I'm late,' Perizada whispered to Billy. 'I had a puncture.' She wore a rainbow-coloured dress with a flared skirt that swirled and caught the sun every time she moved, a bright red and yellow headscarf tied back behind her hair and a gold hoop dangling from each ear.

'You look like a real gipsy,' Billy said, 'an' not a bit like a witch.'

Perizada laughed. 'Thank you, Billy.'

In no time, the garden filled up with people, and Billy was pleased to see a queue, headed by Mrs Lavender Baggit, at the caravan to see Perizada. He thought it was more to do with curiosity about the fortune-teller than wanting to know what their fate was.

Danny's brother Tim produced a drawing pad and offered to sketch portraits, at half-a-crown a go, if anyone was interested. 'He's a brilliant artist,' Danny told everyone proudly. 'If it hadn't been for the war, he'd have probably been famous by now.' Despite half-a-crown being more than they could afford, a queue of mothers wanting Tim to draw their children, lined up at his stall.

Billy saw Doctor Bainbridge and went over to ask him to buy a raffle ticket. He bought five. 'I could do with some extra sugar,' he said. 'And how are you, Billy? Is your back better now?'

'Yes, thank you, Doctor Bainbridge. 'My mum says it was the herb medicine you gave us.'

'Ah, yes,' Doctor Bainbridge said. 'That was one of Perizada's concoctions. Wonderful woman is Perizada, though you wouldn't think so if you listened to what some folk have to say about her.'

Billy pointed to the caravan where there were still people waiting, 'She's telling fortunes,' he said. 'Over there.'

'Well I never,' the doctor said. 'She's certainly popular this morning.'

Mrs Lavender Baggit wandered around trying to find someone to tell about how displeased she was with Perizada's warning to be careful what she had to say about a certain person in the village. 'One and thruppence_wasted,' she grumbled to Billy. 'I've never said a bad word about anyone in my life. And why that woman was asked to come here and peddle her nonsense, I shall never know.'

Billy smiled. 'Want to buy some raffle tickets, Mrs Baggit?' he said. 'There's a bag of sugar for the winner.'

Mrs Baggit gave him a black look. 'I have no intention,' she said, 'of parting with any more money, and will be going home forthwith.' As she turned away and marched to the gate with her nose in the air, something very strange happened. In an otherwise clear sky, the appearance as if from nowhere of a black cloud, startled everyone and the gentle breeze turned without warning into a roaring gust of wind. It swooped down over the garden, caught Mrs Baggit's hat, lifted it off her head into the air and bore it away over the tops of the trees and out of sight. Billy looked across to where Perizada watched with amusement as she sat on the steps of the caravan, puffing away at her clay pipe, her face the picture of innocence. *She* made that gust of wind happen, he thought. She *is* a witch.

Mrs Baggit screamed for someone to go and rescue her best hat. 'Don't just stand there,' she yelled at Billy. 'Go after it, you stupid boy.' He ran through the gate, along the Avenue and into Woodsmoke Lane, but the hat was nowhere to be seen. Then he saw Jethro Quirke staggering towards him, whisky bottle in one hand and walking stick in the other.

'Have you seen a lady's hat floating around?' Billy asked the old man.

Jethro Quirk's bloodshot eyes bulged. 'No, I have not,' he said in his broad, Irish accent, 'seen any hats floating around lately. And while I might take more whisky than is good for me, I have not yet started seeing things.' He moved closer to Billy. 'And I've a good mind to clip your ear for you, you impudent young rascal, for making fun of me.'

Billy didn't stop long enough to have his ear clipped but ran on and was just about to give up the search when he spotted something lying in the hedge at the side of the lane. It was the hat, minus its cherries. 'Well,' he said aloud to himself, 'I'm not going to waste time looking for *those*.'

He ran all the way back to the fete where an enraged Mrs Baggit, looking as if she would burst, was yelling at Perzada. 'I always said you were a witch,' she screamed. '*You* with your jiggery pokery are to blame for what happened. You put a curse on me, you did.'

Perizada carried on puffing gently at her pipe. 'I tells folk the truth,' she said. 'An' if they don't like it, it iddn't my fault.'

'Your hat, Mrs Baggit,' Billy said, handing her what was left of it. 'The cherries must've come off somewhere but I couldn't find them.'

The angry woman snatched it from him and, without another word to anyone, stormed off into The Avenue. Perizada gave Billy a wicked smile before going back to her fortune telling.

By twelve o'clock, the crowd had dwindled to just a few, and the fete closed.

'Did you have your fortune told?' Billy asked his mother as they were clearing up.

'No, I didn't.'

'Why not, Mum?' He was disappointed. He'd hoped his mother would meet Perizada so that she could see for herself that there was nothing to worry about.

'For one thing,' she said, 'I couldn't leave Shirley on her own and for another, I don't want to know what is going to happen in the future, in case it's bad news.'

Billy glanced towards the caravan. 'Well, you can still meet her,' he said. 'She's coming over.'

The two women smiled at each other and Doris Parkin thanked Perizada for coming. 'It meant a lot to everyone,' she said, glancing at Billy.

Perizada smiled. 'I've enjoyed it.' She handed Billy a bag of money and bent to whisper in his ear. 'Look in old Jethro Quirk's front garden for the cherries,' she said. Then, before anyone could say anything else, she made off on her bicycle along the Avenue.

'Strange woman,' his mother said. 'What was she whispering about?'

'Nothing much, Mum,' Billy said. It wouldn't do to tell her that Perizada was, after all, a bit of a witch.

Once everyone had cleared the garden, they all went inside the house, where Sam's dad counted the money. After about half-an-hour, a loud cheer went up as he announced that they had raised six pounds, twelve shillings and two pence.

'Danny's dad will take it into the bank on Monday and arrange for a cheque to be sent to Mrs

Clementine Churchill who will, I'm sure, be very pleased with that,' he said.

Doris Parkin won the draw and as she accepted her prize bag of sugar, a thought came to her about what she could do with the abundance of fruit there was in the orchard. At teatime, around the table, she told them all of her plans for the sugar she'd won. 'There is so much fruit in the orchard,' she said, 'that lots of it will go rotten and have to be thrown away.' She held up her prize. 'I thought that if we all take saccharin in our tea, I could use this and our sugar ration to make jam.'

Billy and Jess pulled faces.

'Saccharin's horrible,' Billy said. 'I don't want it in *my* tea.'

'Nor me,' Jess agreed.

'I don't mind,' Shirley said, giving Billy and Jess a sly look. She loved getting her own back on them. 'I like jam.'

'Where will you get jam jars from?' Billy asked, hoping his mother hadn't seen them for sale in the village for a halfpenny each. No jam jars ... no jam, and no saccharin.

'There's a shop in the village that sells them,' Shirley piped up. 'I saw them the other day.'

Billy gave her a dark look and Jess said, 'little sneak. *I've* never seen any, have *you* Billy?'

'No,' Billy lied. Of course he'd seen empty jam jars for sale in the old general store on Horndean Hill, but wasn't going to admit it. He wasn't fond of jam very much and didn't like saccharin at all.

They'd all tried it once before and it had made the tea taste horrible.

'I tell you what,' their mother said. 'It's your birthday next week Jess, so we'll go shopping in Horndean. You can choose your present, and we can see what we can find in the way of empty jam jars.'

After tea, Billy went to look for Mrs Baggit's cherries. How did Perizada know they were in old Quirk's front garden? He found a stick and poked around in the tangle of weeds and bushes but found nothing but a couple of empty whisky bottles and some old bits of newspaper. Perizada must have been pulling his leg.

'What you pokin' around in my garden for?'

Billy jumped at the sound of Jethro Quirk's voice.

'The cherries off that straw hat,' Billy said. 'I think they went in your front garden.'

The old man leaned on his stick. 'Aint you got eyes in your head?' he said, pointing to the ground at Billy's left foot. 'There they are. Now buzz off.'

Mrs Baggit snatched the cherries from Billy's hand. 'That woman Perizada is an evil witch,' she said, without even thanking him for finding them. 'An' if I had my way, she'd be drummed out of this village once and for all.'

Billy gave the angry old woman a look but said nothing. Perizada had, he knew, used some sort of magic to get her own back on the village gossip and that could only mean that she *is* a witch of one kind or another. Either that or she had some special powers. It didn't really matter to him. What Perizada had done hadn't hurt anyone, and the sight of Mrs Baggit's face, all puckered and red with anger was reward enough.

Chapter Fifteen

In Danger

On the morning of Jess's eleventh birthday, Billy said at breakfast that he was off for the day with the Woodlarks. 'Boys only – girls not invited.'

'I don't care,' Jess said. 'Mum's taking me shopping to buy my present.'

'Another stupid book about girls' boarding schools I suppose?'

'Yes, if you must know. I *like* Angela Brazil stories so mind your own business, Billy Parkin.'

'That's enough you two,' their mother said. 'You just watch what you're getting up to, Billy. And be back here for tea.'

'*Yes*, Mum.' He packed some fresh fruit and biscuits into a paper bag and set off to call for Danny and Sam.

The day with the Woodlarks turned out to be a bit of a flop. Danny turned up but Sam had to help his dad build a chicken run. Billy had found a length of stout rope in the garden shed, and they tied a loop in the end, big enough to put their legs through. Then they secured the other end to the branch of an oak tree so that they could swing across to the other side of the dell. They took turns mimicking Tarzan's call as they swung back and fore, yelling "Aaah-eee-aaah-eeee" at the top of their voices. Billy closed his eyes when it was his turn and tried not to think about what could happen if the rope gave way. The ground beneath him dipped into a large hollow and seemed a long way away, and he felt a bit sick.

Then old Jethro Quirk appeared at the bottom of his garden. 'Take that noise somewhere else, you pair of hooligans,' he hollered, 'or I'll come over there an' take me stick to you, so I will.'

'We're not doing any harm,' Billy answered back, noticing how unsteady the old man was on his feet.

'Oh, yes y'are,' Quirk said. 'Now clear off.'

'Miserable old spoilsport,' Danny shouted as they ambled back to his cottage, where his mother gave them a glass of lemonade. They told her about Mr. Quirk spoiling their fun.

Well, I must say,' she said, 'you were making a terrible din out there. And he *is* an old man, don't forget.'

'*Yes*, Mum, 'Danny said, rolling his eyes at Billy.

Billy left soon after that. There was nothing to do for just the two of them and he may as well get on with one of his favourite books. He liked reading Biggles, or Just William, not daft things like stories about posh schools for girls by Angela Brazil. First, though he wanted to have a look around part of the woods he'd not seen before.

A gate at the end of Danny's back garden led to where the woods thickened and Billy found a piece of stick with which to separate the mass of brambles almost covering the narrow footpath between the trees. He could hear all kinds of strange noises; rustlings in the undergrowth, the flapping of wings in the trees and the sound of mice scurrying over the leaves on the ground. He jumped as a rabbit sat up on its hind legs and raised its ears. It looked at him from frightened eyes and then darted away, its white scut (tail) bobbing as it disappeared into the bushes. He walked on. The density of the trees had cut out the sunlight so that he now found himself in heavy shade. With no idea where he was, he began to feel nervous. The hairs on the back of his neck stood up and he could feel his heart racing as he became aware that someone or something was watching his every move. Apart from a rundown old shack, he could see no sign of human life in this part of the woods. A feeling of panic gripped him, and he decided to try to find his way home.

In a small clearing, lightened by the sun's rays, he came across three pathways, each going off in a different direction. He scratched his head and thought about it. They all looked the same and he couldn't make up his mind which one to take. The feeling that he was not alone was stronger than ever here. He closed his eyes and turned around in a circle. Whichever path he was facing when he opened them again, he would follow.

'Don't move.'

Billy's eyes flew open and he stood frozen with fear to the spot.

'You move and I shoot.'

Billy had heard that voice somewhere before. He stayed quite still for a minute or two and then, from behind a tree a man stepped out onto the path and stood pointing what looked like a revolver at him. It was Ernst Hartmann, the German airman Billy had helped capture a few weeks ago.

'W-what are you doing here?' Billy said. He broke out in a cold sweat and shook with fear as the German came closer.

'I am – as you stupid English say – on the run,' Hartmann said, keeping the gun trained on Billy. 'I vant food. And drink.'

Billy had often wondered what had happened to the German airman. He'd heard that some prisoners of war were being used to help out on farms, and there were several around Horndean. Hartmann must have been working on one of them.

'I can't get food,' he said.

Hartmann raised the gun. 'You will get food or I come to your cottage and shoot everyone.'

A picture of his mum and dad and sisters, all peppered with bullet holes, and lying dead in Railway Cottage, rose before Billy's eyes. 'You won't escape,' he said. 'You'll get caught, you will.'

'Not if you help me.'

'I *can't*.'

The gun was now inches away from Billy's nose, and Hartmann had an evil look on his face. He indicated with a flick of the weapon for Billy to move. 'I vill follow,' he said. 'You get food and drink. I kill you all if you tell anyone. Remember that.'

'You won't get far,' Billy said as he picked his way through the woods, Hartmann at his heels, the gun now trained on his back.

When Danny's cottage came into view, Hartmann ordered Billy to stop. 'I haf to stay here,' he said. 'You get food. And don't forget. You tell anyone and,' he pointed the pistol towards Woodsmoke Lane, 'bang! You are all dead.' He crouched down into the undergrowth, covering himself with foliage.

Billy ran the last few yards through the trees into the lane. Whatever food he helped himself to, his mother would find out it was missing. Most things were on ration, and she always knew exactly what was in her larder. He let himself in through the back door to find that she wasn't yet back from her shopping trip to the village. The larder contained a loaf of bread, some margarine, a pot of jam and some porridge oats. There were tins of stuff but that wouldn't be of any use to Hartmann. He cut a thick slice off the end of the loaf, spread it with margarine and jam and wrapped it in a sheet of newspaper. A basket of fruit on the floor yielded some plums and apples. He filled a paper bag with some of each then took an empty milk bottle and topped it up with water.

Hartmann snatched the food from Billy's trembling hands and ate it greedily. He'd not eaten since this morning; when he'd made a run for it from Franklin's farm, in nearby Clanfield, where he'd been helping out. 'Soon,' he said to Billy, 'the farmer will see that I am missing and send out a search party. The English; they are fools.'

'You won't escape,' Billy said, wishing now that he'd gone straight home from Danny's.

Hartmann waved the gun in the air. 'I vill. And you are going to help me. I am not going to stay in this stupid country until Germany wins the war. I go home to see my wife, and no one is going to stop me,' he said. Hartmann finished off the last piece of fruit, and swallowed the water in one gulp

'I've got to go home now,' Billy said. 'My mum will be … '

'You not going anywhere,' Hartmann said, still clutching the gun in one hand.

'But...'

'Shut up.' Hartmann clapped a hand over Billy's mouth. 'Someone is coming.'

'Billeeee, Billeee, where are you?' Shirley's voice echoed through the trees.

Billy felt Hartmann's hand tighten over his mouth.

'Call her over here,' he ordered. 'Go on. She vill be useful to me.' He took his hand away and Billy tried to make a run for it but Hartmann dragged him back by his collar.

'You leave her alone,' Billy said, 'she's only five.' He felt the gun between his shoulder blades.

'Do as I say.'

Billy had no need to call Shirley. She suddenly appeared between a gap in the undergrowth, and he flapped his hand to warn her to go away, but she didn't take any notice.

'Oh, *there* you are,' she said. 'Mummy sent me to look for you. She forgot to get something in the village and wants you to go.' Her eyes darted from Billy to Hartmann and back again.

Hartmann crouched down and beckoned to her. 'Hello, little fraulein,' he said, holding out a hand. 'Come here.'

Billy shook his head at her. 'Run,' he said, but she ignored him and Hartmann grabbed hold of her arm and pulled her to him.

'That vas a silly thing to say,' he said.

'Leave her alone. Let her go.'

'I will, when you haf gott me more food.' Hartmann reeled off a list of things he wanted Billy to get. 'Then I will let you both go. And remember, you tell anyone and I shoot her,' he pointed at Shirley, who thought it was some kind of game and didn't seem to understand the danger she was in.

Billy watched, terrified as she settled into the crook of Hartmann's arm. With no idea of how he could meet Hartmann's demand for food, he set off home. His mother would be there, and Jess, so how could he raid the larder again without them seeing? And would Hartmann really shoot an innocent little girl if he didn't get what he wanted? Billy didn't think so but you never knew. He crept round the side of the cottage and stopped suddenly at the sight of two policemen and Home Guard Harry Greentree talking to his mother. Billy tried to backtrack but she saw him and told him to stay right where he was.

'Where've you been?' she asked. 'And where's Shirley?'

If he told the truth, Shirley would be in danger. 'Been playing in the woods, and no, I haven't seen her,' he lied. He felt Harry Greentree's eyes on him and could tell the Home Guard man knew he wasn't telling the truth. He and the policemen must be searching for the escaped German.

'Come along, son,' one of the policemen said, 'let's have the truth. Where's your sister, Shirley?'

Billy looked at the ground, shifted from one foot to the other and shoved his hands in his pockets, four pairs of eyes watching his every move. He'd have to tell them about Hartmann, and that the German was holding Shirley hostage. 'He's got a gun,' he shouted. 'And he's going to shoot her if I tell ...'

'All right, calm down and don't you worrit about that,' Harry Greentree said. 'It's a toy gun. Hartmann took it from farmer Franklin's boy. Said he was going to mend it or something, and the lad was frightened to tell his dad. Now you jus' show us where they are.'

Billy looked at his mother, and knew from the anger in her eyes that he would be in for trouble once this was all over. She nodded. 'You come straight back here when you've finished. I've a few words to say to you.'

'Yes, Mum.'

He led the way, with Harry Greentree following at a short distance behind, and the two policemen spreading out on either side. They picked their way through the woods, treading carefully so as not to make a noise on the dried bracken. Billy couldn't quite remember where he'd left Hartmann and Shirley and he started to panic. Supposing the German had taken her away and they never found her? Or maybe strangled her and hid her body somewhere. Or … he turned to say something to Harry Greentree, who put a finger to his lips.

'Shh,' he whispered, 'I can hear something.' They both stopped and listened and he waved a hand to each of the policemen to do the same. The sound of a little girl singing echoed through the trees. Shirley loved to sing and it was her voice they could hear.

Billy made to dash forward but Harry Greentree grabbed his arm, and pointed back to the way they'd come. 'You go home,' he mouthed, 'and leave this to us.'

Billy shook his head. 'No, Mister Greentree. I want to go with you.' Shirley might be a spoilt little pest but it was partly *his* fault the German had taken her as hostage, and he, Billy, wanted to help with her rescue. With Harry Greentree and the policemen, he crept forward until they came to a clearing where Hartmann, with Shirley still in the crook of his arm, sat teaching her a German song. He looked up in surprise and sprang to his feet as Billy ran forward and snatched Shirley from his grasp. Before Hartmann could escape, the three men fell on him, two holding him down while the third put him in handcuffs. Billy watched them take him away and then took Shirley home where he knew he had to face the anger of their mother.

'You're banned from leaving this cottage for a week,' she said. 'You are irresponsible and it's about time you grew up. Shirley could have been kidnapped or killed, and so could you.'

'Sorry,' was all Billy could think of to say.

111

Later, he sat on his bed thinking about the day's events. His mother had called him irresponsible, whatever that meant, and that it was time he grew up. All right, so he would be thirteen next January, and leaving school the year after that. But why did mums and dads treat you like a child one minute, and then expect you to act like an adult, the next? He didn't understand grown-ups at all. Anyway, why should he take the blame for something that was Shirley's fault and not his? If she'd run away when he'd told her to, none of it would have happened. Although what would have become of him then? His thoughts turned to Hartmann. Billy was surprised to find that he felt a bit sorry for the German, who would now be sent to a prisoner of war camp instead of enjoying the freedom of working on a farm. And if the war went on for a few more years, as his dad seemed to think, then it would be a long time before Hartmann saw his family again. If at all.

Chapter Sixteen

Dandy the Fox Cub

When Billy went back to school after the summer holidays, he moved up a class and no longer had to sit next to George Bunn. George, who hadn't said one word to anyone since the death of his father, now sat in the front row where the teacher could keep an eye on him. Billy shared a desk at the back with Sam who larked about instead of learning, but Billy didn't mind that as sometimes school could be boring and Sam was a good laugh.

'Why don't you get on the bus?' Sam asked one afternoon as he caught up with Billy, who had set out to walk home.

'Because,' Billy said, 'it's full of stupid girls, like my sister Jess and her friend, Meg. They've just started at Cowplain, and all they do is chatter and giggle. It annoys me, and I'd sooner walk.'

'I'll walk with you, then.'

'Did you pass for the secondary school?' Billy asked as they sauntered along the road towards Horndean.

'Nope, I didn't,' Sam said, 'but I wouldn't have wanted to go anyway. I want to leave school when I'm fourteen and go out to work.'

'I passed,' Billy said, 'but my mum and dad wouldn't let me go. They said they couldn't afford all the things I'd need. I'll have to leave school when

I'm fourteen and take an apprenticeship somewhere so that I can start to earn some money.'

'What sort of 'prenticeship?'

'Woodworking. But I'll have to do what my dad sets up for me.'

'Why can't *you* pick what you want to do?'

Billy shrugged. 'I dunno. It's what dads in Pompey do.'

'Well *I'm* goin' to pick my own job,' Sam said. 'My dad says I can choose. He doesn't mind as long as I find something.'

'So, what d'you want to do?'

'Work on a farm, with animals.'

'That sounds good. Will you be a vet?'

Sam shook his head. 'No. I'd have t'go to college to do that. I just want to be a farmer.'

'Like ole man Franklin?'

'Yes. Can you play Conkers?' Sam said, changing the subject.

'A bit. We had some Chestnut trees in the park near where I lived in Pompey, and sometimes I'd have a game with my friend, Dave Spiller. He got killed in an air raid.'

'Blimey! That must've been rotten.'

'Yeah, it was,' Billy said. 'Anyway, why did you ask me about Conkers?'

'There's a sort've competition at the end of October. Just a few of us from the school, and I can put your name down if you want to join in.'

'I wouldn't be any good,' Billy said.

'It's only a bit of fun. No prizes or anythin'.'

'Oh, all right, then. I'll have a go.'

They parted at Sam's front gate and Billy walked on, deep in thought. Working on a farm sounded much better than making things from wood. Yesterday, he'd overheard his parents talking about going back to Portsmouth, but he liked living in the country, and if they could stay here, maybe *he* could work on a farm. He'd like that. He didn't want to leave Horndean although he knew the time would come when the owners of Railway Cottage would want it back. It wasn't that he'd made many friends here. Danny and Sam were all right except that Danny seemed to think he was better than everyone else because he went to a private school and his father was a bank manager. Billy still missed Dave but as the months went by, the memory of that terrible night when he was killed, had begun to fade. As for George Bunn, well Billy would never be able to make friends with him.

When he reached home, his mother was still out working at the café. She'd promised to always be there for him and Jess but this was the third time he'd arrived home to find the house empty, except for her. It was all right for Shirley. She would have stopped by on her way home from school and had cakes and lemonade at the café, like she always did.

He threw his satchel on the floor, opened the back door and sat on the step. 'Where's mum?' he shouted to Jess.

'She's not home yet.'

'Well, I can *see* that, can't I, stupid.'

Jess ignored him and went on reading her book.

'D'you want to go back to Portsmouth?' he said.

'No.'

'Why?'

Jess sighed and closed her book. 'I don't know,' she said. 'And why d'you think we're going back to Portsmouth anyway?'

'I heard mum and dad talking about it. Dad says we ought to go back soon.'

'You should stop ear-wigging,' she said, picking up her book again. 'You're always listening to what other people are saying. And mum rented the cottage for a year. Remember, Dumbo?'

'Aw. Shut up.' With his elbows resting on his knees and his hands under his chin, Billy sat and thought about why he didn't want to move away from here … ever. After all, there were far more interesting things to do in Pompey, like the Saturday morning picture house, with his favourite cowboy Roy Rogers, and Trigger the horse. Or a Laurel and Hardy film. Then there was the beach, and train-spotting on Fratton Bridge. But best of all, he liked Allaway's fish and chip shop where, for a ha'penny you could get a bag of crispy bits left over from frying the fish. Mr Allaway, who did the frying, also let you sprinkle them with salt and vinegar. Billy's mouth watered at the memory. There was none of that here, and he wouldn't find a wood-working job in Horndean either. And old Horace Skinter at school didn't like him. In his opinion, evacuees were nothing but trouble. Scallywags, and troublemakers, the lot of them. Billy couldn't understand why he, himself, wanted to stay here, and by the time his mother and Shirley arrived home half-an-hour later, he still hadn't worked out why he preferred the countryside to the town.

'I'll go and see Perizada,' he said aloud to himself, 'and see if she can tell me.' He hadn't seen her since the day of the fete and she'd wonder what had happened to him. He'd go next Saturday.

He went out and wandered down the side of the cottage, across the lane and past old Quirk's garden into the woods where he stopped and listened as a soft cry, coming from somewhere in the undergrowth caught his ear. Apart from the fluttering of a few birds as they flew from tree to tree, it was quiet. He looked all around but not seeing anything, walked on, scuffing at the dead leaves covering the ground. Then he heard the noise again and, peering into the undergrowth, met a pair of brown eyes staring up at him from a tangle of bramble bushes. Caught up in them, a cub fox struggled to free itself. Billy knelt down and with a piece of stick, pulled the brambles away from the terrified animal. It didn't move and Billy noticed blood on one of its legs.

The cub looked up at him with frightened eyes, and Billy stood up. 'Can't leave you there, can I?' he said. 'Stay, and don't move. I'll be back.'

He ran down the side of Quirk's shack and across the lane to Railway Cottage. From round the back, he fetched the cart used for collecting books, lined it with an old coat he found in the shed, and went back to fetch the injured animal.

Billy was lying on the floor of the sitting room, trying to get the cub to drink some milk, when his mother arrived home. She nearly blew the roof off. 'Get that thing out of here,' she screamed. '*Now*.'

'Aw, Mum, it's hurt. Look.' Billy held up the injured leg, now cleaned and bandaged. 'He's been attacked by a big dog I think.'

Shirley crouched down and went to pat its head but Doris Parkin swiped her hand away. 'Don't touch it. If it bites you, you'll be poisoned.'

'Don't be silly, Mum. He's not going to bite anyone,' Billy said.

'Well, you can just take it outside to the shed. It's probably full of fleas and it's not staying in here.' She dragged Shirley away from the animal. 'Open the back door for Billy, Jess.'

'There's no room in the shed, 'Billy said.

'Then go and make some.'

Billy scrambled to his feet and stomped out of the back door. 'It'll die if we don't take care of it,' he shouted over his shoulder.'

'Well, if it does,' his mother shouted back, 'there's plenty more where it came from.'

Billy couldn't understand what all the fuss was about. He knew she didn't like dogs, and foxes were almost the same, but there was no need to go on the way she did. He went to the shed and cleared some space in one corner. The old coat he'd found earlier was still in the cart so he took that and laid it on the floor. Then he went back in the cottage to fetch the cub.

'And it's only staying here for tonight,' his mother said as he carried it out to the shed. 'Tomorrow is goes back to the woods where it belongs.'

Billy pulled a face behind her back. She could say what she liked; it wasn't going anywhere until its leg was better.

Later, when his father came in from work, Billy took him to the shed and showed him the cub. 'I want to look after him, Dad, until he's better, but Mum says I've got to let him go back to the woods tomorrow. He'll die.'

Fred Parkin examined the injured leg. 'Don't you worry, Billy,' he said, 'I'll have a word with your mother. It'll be all right, I promise.'

Billy called the cub Dandy after his favourite comic, and by Saturday, Dandy had stopped eating. It would no longer take the bread and warm milk that he offered, turning its head away whenever he tried to feed it from a spoon. It lay on the warm bed in the shed, not moving except to raise its head now and then when it heard his voice. He knelt down beside the sick animal. 'I'm taking you to see my friend Perizada,' he said. 'She'll know what to do with you.' He lifted Dandy and the coat into the cart and set off without a word to his mother. She had been complaining about the fox cub all week and had forbidden Jess and Shirley to go anywhere near it.

Billy was glad that at least his father was on *his* side, otherwise Dandy would have been dead by now.

As he pushed the cart down Potters Lane, he saw Mrs Baggit leaning over her gate. 'What are you up to now, Billy Parkin?' she demanded to know. 'Boys seen roaming around on a Saturday morning with a dead-looking fox in a cart are up to no good.'

'He's hurt his leg,' Billy said, 'and I'm taking him out for a walk.' If he told her he was going to see Perizada, he'd get an earful. Mrs Baggit didn't like him and had never forgiven Perizada for causing her to lose the cherries off her best hat that day at the garden fete, even though she'd got them back in the end.

'Humph!' she said. 'A likely story.'

Billy couldn't ever remember having seen so many hairy chins on one person, and he tried his best not to laugh as she shook her head and set them all moving at once. She peered into the cart at Dandy, then without another word, turned and shuffled down the path to her front door.

Perizada took one look at Dandy. 'There's nothing I can do, Billy,' she said. 'His leg is turning bad and 'tis best to let him die.'

'No!' Billy shouted. 'You make potions to make people better so why can't you give him something?'

'Animals is different, Billy. Them's need special medicine from the vet.'

'I'll give you all my pocket money,' Billy said, desperate to do anything that would save Dandy. 'I've saved up a shilling and you can have that.'

Perizada smiled. 'I tell you what,' she said. 'I'll attend to his leg, and you can have some extract of clover to mix in with his food. T'won't do any good but if it keeps you happy, then that's all right.' She went to one of her many shelves and brought down a tin of black stuff. When she removed the bandage Billy had wrapped around the leg, the smell was so terrible that he had to pinch his nostrils together but Perizada didn't seem to mind. She bathed the wound, then smeared some of the cream over it and covered it in a clean rag. 'I don't want your money, Billy,' she said, handing him the cream and a bottle of purple liquid. 'Put the cream on morning and night, and a teaspoonful of this liquid in his food three times a day and we'll see what happens. I don't think he'll get better though.'

Dandy curled himself into a ball and went to sleep and Perizada poured Billy a cold drink. She stared at him from those strange, green eyes, then, 'sit down a minute,' she said, 'and tell me what's bothering you.'

'I don't want to go back to live in Portsmouth,' he said.

'Oh. Why is that? And who says you're going to?'

'I heard my mum and dad talking about it the other day, but I like living here in the country, an' 'I don't want to go back to a dirty old town.'

'Well, Billy, it be your mum and dad who decides where you all live, and you have to do as they say.'

An idea flew suddenly into his head. 'I could stay here with you, couldn't I?'

Perizada stood up, reached for his hand and pulled him to his feet. 'No, Billy Parkin, you could do no such thing,' she said. 'Whatever would folks think?'

'I don't care.'

'Well, *I* do.'

'I thought you were my friend,' he said, as she moved over to the door and opened it.

'I am, Billy but I'm not your mother. Now, off you go and look after your foxy friend. Let me know how he gets on, won't you?'

'All right.'

'And Billy.'

'Yes?'

She gave him one of her rare smiles. 'I'll miss you if you do go back to Portsmouth,' she said, closing the door on him.

Chapter Seventeen

A Bad Day

Billy read the note one of the other boys had passed to him under the desk. *"Conker competition will be next Wednesday after school in the playground. You're playing George Bunn in the first round,"* it said. He screwed the piece of paper into a ball and went to shove it in his pocket when Horace Skinter, pounced. He held out a hand and demanded to see the note.

'Fancy some more of the cane, Parkin?' he said, pushing his face into Billy's, who tried not to laugh when he noticed a large dewdrop on the end of the teacher's nose.

'No, sir.'

'The passing around of notes in class is not allowed,' Horace Skinter said, wiping the dewdrop away with the back of his hand.

'Yes, sir, I do know that.'

The teacher unscrewed the note and read it. 'I've a good mind,' he said, screwing it up again and throwing it the length of the classroom into the waste paper bin, 'to report you to the headmaster. Not just for passing notes around but for being impudent.'

Billy said nothing. What would be the use? Skinter didn't like him because Skinter didn't approve of evacuees.

'I spoke to you, Parkin.'

Billy found his voice. 'Yes, sir.'

Skinter brought his hand crashing down on the desk. 'One-hundred lines, Parkin,' he said. 'You will stay behind after school today and write out one-hundred times *"I must not pass notes around in class nor be rude to Mister Skinter when he tells me off."*

'But I wasn't ... 'Billy began.'

'Silence!'

A great feeling of injustice welled up inside Billy. It was always the same with the English teacher, who picked on him for the least little thing. Billy hadn't been rude to him at all, and it wasn't fair. He leapt from his seat and stared into Skinter's little piggy eyes. 'I hate you, Skinter,' he shouted. 'Hate you, hate you, hate you!' and to the astonishment of the rest of the class, he fled from the room, slamming the door as he went.

His eyes blinded with tears, he ran along the corridor, straight into the headmaster who was just leaving his office to investigate all the noise he could hear coming from Horace Skinter's classroom. The cup of tea he was holding shot out of his hand and into the air, the contents spilling down the front of his suit, the cup shattering into dozens of pieces as it hit the floor. He grabbed Billy's arm. 'What's going on here?' he said. 'Where do you think you're off to, Parkin?'

Billy wriggled free and ran on, ignoring the headmaster's orders to stop. With no idea where he was heading, he careered along the corridor and out through the double doors at the end, finally coming to a stop at the school gates. Here, he paused for breath for a few minutes before walking quickly to the bus stop. He didn't care if he never went back to Cowplain school ever again. In fact, he'd changed his mind about not wanting to move back to Portsmouth. He'd go tomorrow if it were possible.

When he reached home, his mother wanted to know what he was doing there at half past three when school didn't finish until four o'clock. Billy told her a lie.

'I came top in my English composition,' he said, 'and Mister Skinter said I could go home early as a reward.' He could tell she didn't believe a word of it by the funny way she looked at him.

He went outside to the shed to see Dandy. The fox cub seemed to be getting better on Perizada's potions, and Billy had been able to remove the bandage from its injured paw. 'You'll be able to go back to the woods soon,' he said, 'but I'll miss you when you've gone.' He patted Dandy's head, and the cub fox closed its eyes. ''I'd keep you if I could but I know my mum wouldn't let me. I don't know what I'm goin' to do, Dandy,' he went on. 'If I go back to school tomorrow, I'll get the cane but if I don't, the school beak'll be after me an' then I'll be in more trouble. It's all that old Skinter's fault. He doesn't like me because I come from Pompey, an' he's always pickin' on me.' Dandy opened one eye, looked at Billy, then curled into a ball and went to sleep.

'Billy … Billeee.' His mother's voice carried across the garden, and she sounded angry. 'Get in here, at once.'

As he reached the kitchen door, she grabbed hold of his arm and pulled him inside. 'What's the meaning of this?' Billy's heart sank into his boots when he saw the portly figure of Walter Cotton, the school attendance officer, sitting in a chair, pen poised over a notebook. 'You told me that Mister Skinter had sent you home for coming top in English.'

Billy studied his toecaps and remained silent.

'Well?'

'He … that Mister Skinter, said I was rude to him. And I *wasn't*.'

'So, according to Mister Cotton here, you ran away from school, knocking a cup of tea all over the headmaster and breaking his best china cup as you went?'

'Yes.' Billy raised his head and looked from his mother to Walter Cotton. 'Skinter hates me, an' I'm not goin' back, so *there*.'

Walter Cotton, who had been making notes, now drummed his fingers on the table. 'I'm afraid, Parkin, that you have no choice in the matter. Perhaps you'd like to tell me a little more about you and Mister Skinter, who I believe is an excellent teacher, devoted to his pupils.'

Billy had to smile at that, and his mother gave him one of her dark looks. 'It was all George Bunn's fault,' he began.

'George Bunn? What has he to do with this?' Walter Cotton asked.

'Me an' George Bunn had a fight in the playground,' Billy told him, 'an' old Skinter took me to the headmaster. I got two strokes of the cane. It wasn't fair,' he went on. 'Old Skinter blamed me for everythin' and let George Bunn off.'

'*Mister* Skinter to you, Parkin.' Walter Cotton carried on making notes. 'And?'

'He picked on me again yesterday an' said I had been rude an' had to stay behind after school and write out a hundred lines.'

Walter Cotton closed his notebook and stood up, and his head almost touched the ceiling. 'As I see it, Parkin,' he said, 'this is a great fuss about nothing. Tomorrow, you will go back to school and apologise for your bad behaviour.' He looked down on Billy. 'Think yourself lucky that the school cares enough about you to send me here to make sure you arrived home safely. The villagers of Horndean have always made newcomers feel welcome and this business of you being "picked on" because you are an evacuee is all in your head. D'you hear me?'

'Yes, Mister Cotton.' Billy wanted to kick him in the shins.

'And let's hear no more of this nonsense.' Walter Cotton turned to Billy's mother. 'Make sure he goes back to school tomorrow, Mrs Parkin,' he said, 'otherwise you and your husband will have to answer to the authorities.'

'Don't worry, he'll be there,' she said as she let him out.

Billy made for the back door. 'Oh, no you don't,' she said. You're not going anywhere until I've had another word with you.'

'What've I done *now*?' Billy slumped into a chair where he sat with his arms dangling between his knees, and looked at the floor.

She disappeared for a minute before returning with Shirley.

'What's *she* doing home from school?' Billy asked.

'*This* is why she isn't at school,' his mother said, lifting Shirley's vest to show her bare chest covered in angry-looking red spots. 'These are flea bites, and she got them from that animal you've been keeping in the shed.'

Billy shot out of his chair. 'That's a lie,' he shouted. 'She got them from that mangy cat of hers. I've seen it scratching itself. Scratch, scratch, scratch – all the time it does it, an' Shirley never goes anywhere near Sandy 'cos *you* won't let her.'

'You leave Raffles alone,' Shirley yelled, bursting into tears.

'Aw, shut up, you big cry baby.'

'That's enough,' their mother said. 'Tonight, Billy, you are to take that animal back to where it came from, and no arguments.'

Billy made for the door. 'I'm goin' out,' he said, almost falling down the steps in his eagerness to get away.

'You come back here, Billy.'

'No!' he stomped off down the side of the cottage and through the gate. 'I'm goin' to see my friend.'

'*Billy.*' The whole lane must have heard his mother's voice.

He turned round to see her standing, hands on hips, on the path. Then he did something he'd never done to his mother before. He blew the longest, loudest raspberry he could manage, and then ran all the way to Potter's Lane. As he passed Mrs Baggit's cottage, she appeared at her gate.

'And where are you off to?' she asked. 'As if I didn't know.'

Billy, who seemed to have taken leave of all his senses, called out to her over his shoulder. 'Mind your own business, you nosey old bat,' he said, almost colliding with Perizada who happened to be wheeling her bicycle into her front garden.

She stared at Billy, her green eyes twinkling. 'I heard what you just said to Mrs Baggit,' she said, and Billy detected laughter in her voice. 'You're a bad boy, Billy Parkin, and no mistake.'

He followed her up the path to the front door.

'I suppose,' she said, inviting him inside, 'you've been up to something again and want to tell me about it?'

She made him a drink of cowslip cordial and, starting from the beginning of what had been a very bad day, he told her everything. Even about the raspberry he'd blown to his mother.

'*Billy*, how could you?' she said. 'B'tween that and what you just called out to Mrs Baggit, you're going to be in real trouble when you get home. She's bound to go and tell your mum.'

Billy didn't care. The day couldn't get any worse, anyway.

'I do think,' Perizada said, 'that you should take Dandy back to the woods now that he's better. Otherwise, you won't be able to get rid of him at all.' She went to one of her cupboards and took out a small tin. 'Here,' she said, 'take this home for your little sister. It'll clear them spots up in no time. And tell your mum that you're sorry for what you did. She'll be all right, you'll see. Mums always are.'

'Thanks, Perizada.' He noticed a photograph on the wall, of a young soldier. 'Do you have any children?' he asked.

Perizada laughed. 'Goodness me, no,' she said. 'I never married. I would have liked to have had some but fate decided otherwise.'

'Why was that?'

Perizada walked over to the window and stared into the garden. 'You're just as nosey as that Mrs Baggit,' she said, turning to face him. 'Still, no harm in telling you, I suppose. When I was a young girl, I had a man friend and we were going to get married at the end of the Great War. That's his picture on the wall. He went off to France and got himself killed at the Somme. I never did meet anyone else, and here I am, a crusty old maid, living alone with my lotions and potions.'

'You're not crusty, Billy said.

'Thanks, Billy. I always think that whatever will be, will be and we can't do anything to change fate.' She sat down. 'Now, about the villagers. They're a kindly lot of folk really and I don't think they have anything against you just because you're an evacuee.'

'But they don't like *you*,' Billy said.

'Ah, but 'tis not that they don't like me. They think I'm some kind of a witch and are a bit scared of me, that's all.'

'Why?' he asked. '*I'm* not scared of you.'

'I suppose it's because I have certain powers, and can do things other folks can't,' she said.

'Like tell fortunes, and stir up a wind?' he said, laughing as he remembered the fete and Mrs Baggit's hat.

Perizada joined in the laughter. 'Something like that, yes.'

'Well, old Skinter doesn't like me, and neither does George Bunn.'

Perizada rose from her chair. 'That's just two people out of a few thousand,' she said, wisely. 'You don't have to take any notice of *them*. And now, Billy Parkin, it's time you went home and made it up with your mum.'

As he passed Mrs Baggit's gate, he was glad to see that she'd gone indoors. Or maybe she'd gone to Railway Cottage to tell his mum about him? He had a horrible pain in his stomach, and a feeling that his bad day wasn't yet over. He ambled round the back of the cottage to face his mother, who was in the kitchen getting dinner. The smell of lamb stew made his mouth water.

'Hello, Mum,' he said, 'that smells good.'

She turned an angry face to him and pointed a finger at his bedroom door. 'In there,' she bawled. 'And I don't want to see you again 'til morning.'

'But …'

'No "buts". I've just had Mrs Baggit at the front door, ranting and raving about some name or other you called her.'

'Well, she's always spying on me. An' she *is* a nosey old …'

'That's enough. Now get in your room and stay there.'

Billy stormed off into his bedroom, flung himself on the bed and fought back the tears. Not because he was a cry baby, but at the unfairness of it all. A bit later, he heard his father come in, and his mother going on and on about what a troublesome boy Billy had become now that he was nearly thirteen.

'If it's not one thing, it's another,' she complained. 'There's always *something*.'

'Where is he now?' his father said.

'I've sent him to bed without his dinner, and told him to stay there 'til morning.'

It all went quiet for a minute or two, then Billy heard his father say, 'Come on, Doris, you can't send the boy to bed hungry. Put him up a plate of stew and I'll take it in and have a word.'

Billy brightened up. He loved his mother's lamb stew. It was nearly all vegetables of course, because meat was on ration, but all the same, even thinking about it made his mouth water. And it would be nice to see his dad, who worked such long hours that he was hardly ever at home.

The door opened and his father appeared. 'Here, Billy,' he said. I've persuaded your mother to let you have some dinner.'

'Thanks, Dad.' Billy said.

'And what's all this I hear about you calling Mrs Baggit names?'

Billy stared into his plate of stew, and then told his father everything that had happened that day.

'Well,' Fred Parkin said eventually, 'you're going to have to say you're sorry to everyone, including Mrs Baggit.' He pointed to Billy's plate. 'Now eat that up before it goes cold, and when you've finished, you can go round to see her. And tomorrow, you're to go back to school and start all over again. All this business of people not liking you because you come from Portsmouth is silly. Your sisters don't seem to have any trouble.'

'All right, Dad,.' Billy promised, wiping his plate clean with a slice of bread.

'And,' his father added, 'We'll take the fox cub back to the woods on Sunday.'

Mrs Baggit was leaning over her gate as usual, when Billy turned into Potter's Lane. He didn't see why he should say he was sorry, but he'd promised his dad. 'I've come to apolo ... apolo ... say I'm sorry, Mrs Baggit,' he said.

She folded her arms and squinted at him from her beady little eyes. 'All right, Billy Parkin,' she said, 'I'll overlook it this time but if it happens again, you'll be in trouble. *Mouthy little boys* I do not like.'

Billy clenched his fists together. He hated anyone calling him a little boy now that he was nearly thirteen.

Chapter Eighteen

Saying Sorry

When Billy went back to school the following morning, the other boys, except George Bunn, treated him as if he were a hero. 'We all had a good laugh yesterday, when old Skinter's back was turned,' Sam told him. 'We heard all about it and nearly *everyone* says you oughta have a medal for what you did.'

'Yeah. An' now I've got to tell him I'm sorry, and I'm not,' Billy said. He told Sam about the incident with Mrs Baggit.

'Blimey!' was all Sam could think of to say.

At half-past-nine, Billy found himself once more in the headmaster's office. Horace Skinter stood with his back to the window. 'Well,' James Armitage said, 'what have you to say for yourself, Parkin?'

Billy shuffled around a bit. 'I'm sorry, sir,' he muttered, looking at his feet.

'Look at me when I'm talking to you.'

Billy raised his head. 'I said I'm sorry, sir,' he repeated. 'I didn't mean to knock tea all down your suit an' break your cup.'

'Not only did you do that, but you also insulted Mister Skinter here,' the headmaster said. He gave a deep sigh and shook his head. 'What *am* I to do with you, Parkin?'

'The cane,' Horace Skinter said, his mean little face lighting up at the thought. 'Six strokes this time, I think.'

The headmaster pointed to a chair. 'Do sit down, Mister Skinter', he said, 'and let's discuss this in a civilised manner.'

Billy almost laughed at the look on Skinter's face.

'First of all, Parkin, you'd better apologise to Mister Skinter,' the headmaster went on. 'I do not put up with pupils being rude to my teachers.'

Billy swallowed on the anger building up inside him. 'Sorry, Mister Skinter,' he said.

Horace Skinter gave Billy a false smile. 'Now, regarding the cane, Mister Armitage?' he said. 'I think we should get it over and done with.'

The headmaster held up one hand. 'No, Mister Skinter. On this occasion, it will not be necessary.' He turned to Billy. 'This is your last chance, Parkin,' he said. 'If you get into any more trouble, then I shall have no option but to do as Mister Skinter suggests. Now go back to your class, and in future, please try to keep out of trouble.'

'Yes, sir.'

Billy didn't go straight back to his classroom. Instead, he pressed himself against the wall by the open door of the headmaster's office and listened.

'I think,' he heard him say, 'that you must be a little more tolerant towards Parkin, Horace.'

'He's an insolent little beggar,' Horace Skinter replied.

'Well, I find him quite a pleasant boy,' the headmaster said. 'I know your feelings about evacuees, but Parkin isn't one in the true sense of the word as he's with his family from Portsmouth, which is but a few miles' away. And don't forget what the boy went through before coming here. I've heard all about the machine-gunning, and how he lost his friend in an air raid. We really must be more tolerant.'

'I would still have given him the cane.'

'Yes, I know you would, but I felt differently. Now go back to your class and try to get on with the boy. After all, he's top of the class in English and I'd have thought that would have … '

The headmaster's voice trailed off as Billy, a big grin on his face, scarpered back to his classroom.

'How many strokes did you get *this* time?' George Bunn asked as he passed George's desk.

'None.'

'You said that last time. You aint half a liar, Billy Parkin.'

On Sunday evening, Billy and his dad took Dandy back to the woods. Dandy could walk now, but Billy decided it would be best to take him in the cart and then let him go. 'Where shall be leave him?' he asked, wondering if the fox cub would follow them back home. Then there would be trouble from Billy's mother.

'We'll take him as far as we can,' his father said, 'where he will be able to pick up the scent of his family.'

'S'posing they've gone and he can't find them?'

'I hope that doesn't happen, Billy because I've promised your mother we would get rid of him. If he comes back home, she'll go mad.'

'I wish she'd let me have a dog', Billy said. Although he felt sad at having to let Dandy go, he was glad it meant having the company of his father for a change.

'That won't happen, Billy,' his father replied. 'Your mother doesn't like dogs, and it would be wrong for us to have one. And she'll never change her mind, so best forget it, eh?'

'I s'ppose so.' They walked on in silence for a few minutes. Then Billy said, 'Why are you always at the dockyard, Dad?'

'Because there's a war on, Billy, and the dockyard's an important part of it.'

'Oh. Are we going back to Pompey soon?'

'Not just yet. We did think about it but there are still air raids over Portsmouth. Your mother wants to go back and look at the house though. Just to make sure everything's all right.' By this time, they were well into the deepest part of the woods. 'I think this'll do,' he said, stopping at a clearing close to where Billy thought he'd found Dandy.

Between them, they lifted Dandy out of the cart. The fox cub wandered around, sniffing the undergrowth, then sat down, curled into a ball and went to sleep. 'What do we do now, Dad?' Billy said.

'Leave him here. He'll be all right.'

Billy noticed that Dandy had one eye open. 'He's not really asleep, Dad,' he said. 'I don't think he wants us to leave him.'

Fred Parkin laughed. 'Foxes are cunning little devils,' he said. 'We'll walk away and see what happens. Come on.'

When they had gone about fifty yards, Billy looked round. Dandy was standing up, with his head on one side, watching them. 'Oh, *look*, Dad,' he said, 'he wants to come back with us.'

'No.'

'*Please.*'

'I said "no" and I mean it. Now come on, it's getting dark.' They walked on.

'I just want one more look,' Billy said, 'jus' to make sure.'

'Go on then.'

Billy turned round again. Dandy had gone.

'He must've found the scent,' Billy's dad said. 'He'll be all right, I promise.'

'Danny's been looking for you,' Jess said, when they arrived home.

'What did he want?'

'I don't know.'

'Why didn't you ask him, you little twerp?'

'Don't you call me names, Billy Parkin, just because you had to get rid of that mangy fox.'

'That's enough,' their mother ordered. 'You can go over and see what he wants, if you like, Billy.'

When Billy went out into the lane, he met Danny on his way back to see him. 'My Auntie Dorothy – the one who is in charge of the village hall – wants the Woodlarks to go to her house for tea,' he said.

'What for? Billy asked.

'I don't know, but will you and Jess come?'

Billy's couldn't think of anything except Dandy. 'I s'pose so,' he said, without interest. 'Depends when it is.'

'Please yourself,' Danny said. 'Why are you in such a bad mood?'

'Aw, leave me alone, Danny.' Billy turned away and began to walk home. 'We'll come to your auntie's tea party,' he called over his shoulder.

'You'd better call for me first then I can show you where she lives,' Danny shouted back. 'It's not next Saturday but the one after. Three o'clock.'

Billy ambled down the side of Railway Cottage and peered into the shed at Dandy's bed where he could see the imprint of the fox cub, and traces of chestnut-coloured hair. Dandy had left behind an unpleasant "foxy" smell, and Billy left the door open to let in some fresh air. He didn't want to listen to his mother going on about *that*. Then he went indoors, straight to his bedroom, and flung himself on the bed. A bit later, he heard his mother call out that supper was on the table, but although hunger pains gnawed at his stomach, he pretended to be asleep.

Chapter Nineteen

The Conker Match

The day before the Conker competition, Billy sat with Sam at dinnertime. 'I don't know anythin' about *real* Conker competitions,' Billy confessed. 'An' I'm playing George Bunn in the first round.'

'He's good,' Sam said. 'He won it last year, and the year before that.'

'Yeah. An' he'll win it again this year, I expect.'

Sam looked around to see if anyone could hear him. 'Don't tell anyone I told you this,' he whispered, 'but there's things you can do.'

'What sort've things?'

'First of all,' Sam said, 'you can make your conkers hard so that they won't break so easy.'

'How?'

'Have you got any old ones from last year?'

'No. Why?'

'Well, they would be nice and hard by now. Anyway, first you have to choose the best ones. Put them in a bucket of water, and then pick out the ones that float, and throw them away. Only use the ones from the bottom of the bucket.'

'That's a lot of fuss just for a game of Conkers,' Billy said. 'What else?'

'Soak them in vinegar all night, or you can bake them in the oven. That'll make them hard as rocks.'

'Is it all right to do that?' Billy asked.

'Yes.'

'Well, why are you whispering then? An' you keep looking around to see if anyone's listenin'.'

Sam went a bit red in the face. 'Well, you're not supposed to do it, but most boys do, an' if you get caught, you just get kicked out, that's all.'

'I wouldn't mind that,' Billy said. 'Then I wouldn't have to play any more games.'

That evening, Billy lined up his best Conkers on the kitchen windowsill. He'd done as Sam had said and soaked them, then picked out the floaters. 'Could I have some of your vinegar, Mum,' he said.

'Whatever for?' she wanted to know, as Billy knew she would.

'If I soak my Conkers in vinegar, it makes them hard.'

'All this seems a bit silly to me,' she said. 'Still, if it keeps you out of mischief, then I suppose it's all right.' She took a bottle of vinegar from the cupboard and handed it to Billy. 'Don't use too much. You can't always buy it in the shops these days.' She gave him an old dish and he put the Conkers in and covered them with the vinegar. Sam had given him a piece of paper with the rules written on it, and Billy studied them carefully. He wanted to beat George Bunn.

Wrap about ten inches of string round your hand and hold it at the height your opponent chooses.

If you miss, you're allowed two more goes.

If the strings get tangled up, the first to call 'strings' gets an extra shot.

If a player drops his conker or his opponent knocks it out of his hand, the other player can shout 'stamps' and jump on it, but if its owner is the first to cry 'no stamps' then it remains intact.

'Crikey!' Billy said aloud to himself. 'I'll never remember all that stuff.'

The following morning, he made a hole through each Conker with a meat skewer, tied a knot in one end of some pieces of string and threaded the other end through. Then he set off for school, his precious Conkers wrapped in a handkerchief.

There were four players from each class, and the competition, held in the school playground under the watchful eye of Charlie Bowen, the school caretaker, began at half-past-four. Billy's game with George Bunn started the match for their class. The two boys faced each other, Conkers at the ready. Billy had won the toss of a coin and had first strike. With the Conker in one hand, string in the other, he drew it back and swung it down to hit George's. He missed.

'You can have another two tries,' Charlie Brown said.

Billy had another go – and missed.

George laughed. 'Come on, Pompey Fleabag,' he said. 'D'you want to borrow someone's glasses so's you can see?'

'That's enough of that,' Charlie Brown said. 'We're not having any name-calling here.'

Billy brought his Conker down so hard that the string unwound itself from his hand and the whole thing fell to the ground. 'No stamps,' he shouted, and the onlookers cheered as George missed his chance to win the round.

The next round didn't go so well for Billy, who had to admit that George *was* an expert at the game. He had hit Billy's Conker so hard that it had cracked, and Billy knew that one more hit and the Conker could fall to bits. The two boys, who were still enemies, stared each other out. Billy took his time to wrap the string around his hand. George held his Conker by its string.

'Too low,' Billy said. 'Hold it up higher.'

George raised the Conker.

'That's *too* high.'

George, looking as mad as a wasp, lowered it.

'Up a little bit,' Billy said, trying not to laugh.

George raised it.

Billy, with his head on one side, eyed it for a bit. 'That's about right,' he said. He clasped his own Conker in his hand. *Thwack*! Not only did it hit George's Conker but also the back of his hand. George let out a cry and the Conker fell to the ground.

'Stamps!' Billy shouted, and jumped on it, grinding it with his heel into small pieces. His own Conker had split almost in two but the string still held it together. George looked as if he were going to cry as a cheer went up from the crowd.

'That was *wizard,*' Sam said to Billy. 'Fancy you knocking ole' George Bunn out've the match.'

'I don't know about that,' Billy said. 'He'll get his own back on me, *I* bet.'

Sam won the next match against a boy called Donald Porter, which left him to fight it out with Billy, who wasn't quite so lucky this time. After missing a hit, Sam had another go and tore Billy's Conker to bits. He was out of the game.

'That'll teach you, *clever dick,*' George said, as Billy went back to the sidelines to watch the rest of the match.

Billy made a face at him. 'Aw, shut up, *you,*' he said.

Sam won the match for their class. Although there were no prizes, he would have his name added to a shield kept in a glass case in the school assembly hall.

'Is that all there is?' Billy said as he and Sam strolled home.

'No,' Sam said. 'I can play on Saturday against the winners of the other classes if I want to.'

'Will you?'

'Oh, I 'spec so. Not much fun just havin' one match, is there?'

'No,' Billy agreed. Secretly, he didn't think that conkers were much fun anyway. 'I might come and watch,' he said.

Chapter Twenty

Visiting Portsmouth

As it turned out, Billy couldn't go to watch the next round of the competition because his mother had decided to visit Portsmouth. When she told him, he complained. 'We're going on Saturday,' she said. 'And before you start, Billy, you are coming with us.'

'Do I have to?'

'Yes, you do. So put your face straight. Your dad can't come as he has to work, and I may need you to give a hand with things.'

'What things?'

She withered him with a look.

They set off early, with Jess complaining about the buses again. 'I'll be sick,' she said. Doris Parkin handed round barley sugar sweets.

'And *I* wanted to wear my best shoes,' Shirley said. 'It's not *fair*.'

'Aw, shut up,' Billy shouted from the back of the bus, where he'd found a seat all to himself.

As the bus chugged down Portsdown Hill, Billy put his nose to the window. He could just make out the pumping station chimney and the tower of the Royal Marine Barracks, outlined against the sky, both of them close to Chessel Road. He blew on the glass and drew a picture of Chad in the steam. "WOT NO BANANAS", he wrote. His mouth watered at the thought of his mother's banana and custard, but she hadn't made it for ages as you couldn't buy them in the shops any more.

'I wonder what our house is like,' he shouted down the bus to his mother.

'Exactly as we left it, I hope,' she replied. 'Your dad has been popping in to keep an eye on it.'

Billy felt just a bit excited at the thought of seeing his old school, and perhaps one or two of the boys from his class.

The first thing he did when they reached Chessel Road was to pull the Anderson shelter door from its hole and peer inside. The smell almost knocked him off his feet. He flashed a torch his mother had insisted he bring with him. 'Crikey, Mum,' he shouted. 'Come an' have a look at this.'

They all crowded around the opening to have a look at the mess. Brown fungi, like giant mushrooms, had grown all over the walls, and the lino that his dad had laid to cover the floor, now floated on top of a pool of stagnant water. The benches where they'd sat during the air raids, were covered in mildew, their legs blackened by the damp. Billy jumped and Shirley screamed as something in a corner moved and ran across the wet carpet.

'It looks like a rat,' Billy said.

'Put the door back and shut it up, Billy,' his mother said, drawing Jess and Shirley away. 'We won't be able to shelter in *there* any more.'

The house felt cold but apart from a thick layer of dust that covered everything, it looked exactly how they had left it six months ago. Doris Parkin went round opening all the windows. 'I think,' she said, 'that we'll have a bit of a clean up. You two girls find a duster each, and Billy will give me a hand to clean the floors.' They set to work and an hour later, the house looked as if they had never left it.

'I want to go out and have a look around,' Billy said. They were sitting round the table drinking the cocoa their mother had made, and eating the sandwiches they'd brought with them.

'I'll come with you,' Jess said.

'Me, too,' Shirley piped up.

'No,' their mother said. 'I'm taking you two to have a look around the shops. Billy can go. But,' she warned him, 'You are to meet us at the bus stop at three o'clock. Is that clear?'

'*Yes*, Mum.'

The first place he made for was his old school, where he sat on a wall and stared at the empty space where Dave had lived. Behind a wire fence, the mounds of rubble and the Anderson shelter had gone, and wild flowers sprouted from the ground, now levelled and made tidy. Someone had made a small wooden cross and leaned it against the remains of one of the walls that were still standing. Billy wanted to read what was on it but, clipped to the fence, a notice, in large, red letters, forbade anyone to enter the site.

'Well if it aint old Billy Parkin.' Billy came out of his daydream at the sound of a familiar voice from behind. He turned round.

'Derek Goode!'

'Yep. An' this is me friend, Mike O'Hagan. You don't know him. He's only just come 'ere to live. His dad's in the Navy.'

Billy jumped off the wall.

'You comin' back to Pompey to live?' Derek said.

'No, not jus' yet. We only came to tidy up the house.'

'Oh. Did you know the headmaster got killed?'

'*No*. When was that?'

Derek looked at Mike. 'A couple of weeks ago, I think, wasn't it? He was on 'is bike goin' home from school, when a bomb fell right in front of 'im. It blew 'im right up in the air, an' he died.'

'I liked him,' Billy said. 'Do you still get *lots* of air raids?'

'Not so many, and most of them in the day.' Derek fumbled in his jacket pocket. 'Want a fag?' he said.

'No, I don't think so, ta,' Billy said. He'd never tried smoking although some of the boys at school had done it.

Derek went up the steps into the school playground. 'Aw. Don't be such a twerp, Billy,' he said, making for the bike sheds. 'No one'll know if we hide over here.'

Billy followed the other two boys into the gloom of the bike shed, and Derek offered a packet of Woodbines around. 'Take a deep breath when you start,' he said, 'an' then blow the smoke out slowly.'

Billy put the cigarette to his lips and inhaled when Derek lit it with a match. It tasted horrible and he had a mouthful of bits of tobacco. He spit them out and drew a deep breath. 'I feel all giddy,' he said, as his head swam so that he could hardly stand up straight.

'That's 'cos it's the first time,' Derek said. 'You 'ave to keep puffin' away at it.'

Billy tried, and then threw the Woodbine to the ground. 'I don't like it,' he said. 'It's makin' me feel sick.'

Mike scrambled to pick up what was left of the cigarette. 'I'll 'ave that,' he said, pressing the lighted end together between his fingers to put it out, and shoving it in his pocket.

Derek finished his, right down to a tiny stub, which he threw over his shoulder into the playground. 'You'll 'ave to learn how to do it, Billy Parkin. *Everybody* smokes,' he said, lighting up another Woodbine. He squinted at Billy through a cloud of smoke. 'I bet you 'aven't kissed a girl, either?'

Billy shook his head. 'Yuk!' he said. 'I don't like girls. They're stupid.'

'What *do* you like, then?'

'Food,' Billy said, without hesitation.

Derek eyed him for a few minutes. 'Girls are nice,' he said. 'I've got one called Sheila.'

'Oh?' Billy was losing interest.

'Yeah.'

'So what.'

'I've kissed her a few times, an' it's nice.'

'So 'ave I,' Mike put in. 'Not Sheila. *My* girl friend's called Norma, an' I've kissed her loads've times.'

'Yeah. Girls like to be kissed,' Derek said.

'What's the time?' Billy asked, changing the subject. He wanted to get away from these two and their talk about kissing girls.

Derek walked across the playground to look at the clock on the school tower. 'Two o'clock,' he called out.

'I'll have to go now,' Billy said. 'We have to catch a bus back to Horndean.'

'All right. We'll see you next time you come 'ome.'

'P'raps,' Billy said.

He walked as far as The Regal cinema, and stood outside, reading the advertisements. They were still showing Tarzan films on a Saturday morning. Today, it was Tarzan Triumphs, and next week, Tarzan's Desert Mystery. It reminded him of Dave, and their Saturday morning trips to the cinema. He crossed the road and sat in the park for a while, thinking about his friend. He still missed him even though it was six months' since he'd been killed. From where he was sitting, Billy could see Allaway's fish and chip shop, and the smell was making him feel hungry. He felt in his pocket to see if he had any money, and pulled out a penny.

'Well, if it isn't young Billy Parkin,' Frank Allaway said, when Billy walked into the shop. 'How are you, son?'

'All right thanks, Mister Allaway,' Billy said.

'Are you back living in Pompey now?'

'No. We've just come for the day.'

'Well, what can I do for you, Billy?'

'Have you got any scraps?'

Frank Allaway lifted the lid of the container at the side of the fryer. 'I think we could find some for you, Billy,' he said, taking a greaseproof bag and filling it almost to the top. He waved away the penny Billy offered. 'Have them for nothing,' he said. 'I was just closing anyway, and they'd have only been thrown away.'

Billy put the penny back in his pocket. 'Thanks, Mister Allaway,' he said. He sprinkled the scraps with salt and vinegar, and then went back to the park. He picked out the biggest bits first, crunched them between his teeth, then licked his lips as fat from the golden, crispy bits of batter, ran down his chin and onto his shirt. His mother would be angry about that but he didn't care. He had almost reached the bottom of the bag when he looked up and noticed a girl he recognised walking towards him. She was small and slim, with lots of dark brown hair tied back with a yellow ribbon, which matched the colour of her coat. Billy thought she looked pretty. He wiped his mouth and hands in his handkerchief.

'Hello, Maureen,' he said.

She sat down beside him. 'Hello, Billy,' she said. 'You back home?'

'No. I came with my mum and sisters jus' to see if the house is all right. They've gone to the shops an' we're goin' back to Horndean later on.'

'D'you like it there?'

'Yeah. It's all right, I suppose.'

'When are you coming back then?'

'When the war's over I 'spec,' Billy said.

They sat in silence for a minute or two, and then Maureen said, 'I've missed you, Billy.'

'Have you?'

'Yes. I remember when you and Dave used to come round to our house to swap comics with my brother, Archie. And sometimes we'd all play Ludo or Snakes and Ladders.'

'Oh, yes. So we did.' Billy was beginning to wish that Maureen would go away. He didn't want to talk about Dave, and what they used to do. 'Where's Archie now?' he said.

'He's evacuated with the Secondary School.'

'Oh. He passed the exam then?'

'Yes, you daft h'aporth. He wouldn't *be* there if he hadn't, would he.'

From where they were sitting, Billy could see the clock above the post office doorway. 'I've got to go now, Maureen or we'll miss our bus, an' my mum'll be mad at me,' he said. They both stood up and Billy remembered what Derek had said about kissing girls. 'Would you let me kiss you?' he said.

'No.'

'Oh, go on.'

'*No*, I said.'

Without thinking, he grabbed hold of her and pressed his mouth on hers. The blow from her hand as she pushed him away and brought it down across his face, almost bowled him over.

'I don't kiss boys, Billy Parkin,' she called over her shoulder as, with her head in the air, she stomped away. 'And you smell of fish and chips. *And* your mouth's all wet.'

'Aw, *shut up*. I always said girls are stupid,' Billy shouted after her. His face was stinging, and he rubbed at it with the back of his hand. Derek Goode could say what he liked. He, Billy, wouldn't be kissing any more girls – not if it meant getting his face slapped.

The wail of the siren brought him to his senses. Minutes later, he looked up into a clear, blue sky where Spitfires and German aircraft were already engaged in a "dog fight" over the city. He watched as they ducked and dived like Dragonflies around a millpond. One aeroplane, its tail alight, spiralled towards earth before exploding in a ball of fire somewhere near the Royal Marine barracks. Billy couldn't tell whether it was a Spit or a German. Then he heard the whistle of a bomb, and before he could drop to the ground, the blast lifted him off his feet and threw him into the air. The bomb landed somewhere behind the Regal cinema, sending a pall of black smoke into the sky. He lay, stunned and breathless, on the gravel path for a few moments and then scrambled to his feet to see an angry air raid warden shaking his fist in the air.

'What d'you think you're doing,' the man bawled. 'Get in this air raid shelter. *Now*.'

Billy, his heart pounding like a drum, ran into the brick-built public shelter on the edge of the park, and sat down. There were only about five people in there – an old man who was swearing because he'd had to leave his dog outside, and a woman with three children.

'Why couldn't you bring your dog in here?' Billy asked the man.

'Because *he* said so,' he replied, pointing to where the air raid warden stood guarding the door.

'Miserable old devil.'

'Yeah.' The old man stood up. 'If I can't bring me best pal in here with me, then I'm off,' he said, barging past the warden to pick up the dog he'd left tied to a lamppost.

Billy heard a babble of voices, and his mother, Jess and Shirley appeared in the doorway. 'Thank goodness you had the sense to come in here, Billy,' Doris Parkin said. 'We had just got back from the shops when that bomb landed, and I wondered what had happened to you.'

'It knocked me over,' Billy said. 'My arm hurts.' He took his jacket off and rolled up his sleeve.

'I can't see in here,' his mother said. 'It'll have to wait until the raid's over.'

When the all clear sounded, they left the shelter and Billy, shading his eyes from the sun, peered across the road. Clouds of black smoke billowed from behind the Regal where the bomb had landed, as crews from two fire tenders battled to bring the fire under control. He wanted to go and have a look but the police were turning everyone away. Just across the road, an old man, clutching a dog's lead, lay still on the pavement.

'Let me have a look at that arm, Billy,' his mother said, as they made their way to the bus stop. The skin from his elbow to his shoulder had begun to turn blue. ''It's badly bruised, and we'll have to get you to doctor Bainbridge when we get home.'

'I'll go and see Perizada,' he said.

'*Yes*, Mum.'

'You'll go and see Doctor Bainbridge.'

'Are we goin' back to live in Pompey after Christmas?' Billy asked, as the bus set off for Horndean.

'No, Billy. I don't think the Germans have finished with Portsmouth yet, so I'm going to ask your dad if we can stay on at the cottage until the summer. Then we'll see.'

'That's good, Mum.'

'I want to go back to Portsmouth,' Shirley said.

'And me,' Jess put in.

Billy rolled his eyes. 'Aw, why do girls *always* have t'be so stupid?' he said.

That evening, Doctor Bainbridge examined Billy's arm, which had now turned a deep shade of purple. 'No bones broken,' he said, 'but you'll have to wear a sling for a little while, and bathe it with witch hazel to bring the bruise right out.'

'I don't know what it is about you, Billy,' his mother said as they walked home from the doctor's surgery. 'You always seem to get into one scrape or another.'

'Wasn't my fault,' Billy said, feeling proud of the fact that his injury was on show for everyone to see. 'Will I have to stay away from school?' he asked, hopefully.

'Certainly not,' his mother replied.

Chapter Twenty-One

Tea at the Hatton Lodge

Danny's Auntie Dorothy lived in a mansion. Well, that's what Billy thought it was when he arrived at Hatton Lodge with Jess, Meg, Danny, Sam and Nancy on the following Saturday afternoon. The house stood by itself on a hill overlooking the village. It had so many windows that Billy couldn't count them all, and a wide driveway on which was parked two cars. The garden stretched as far as the eye could see, and there were three horses in a paddock to the side of the house.

'Blimey!' he whispered to Jess, as they scrunched up the gravel drive, 'she must have pots of money.'

A large lady, dressed in the dark green suit and maroon shirt of the W.V.S., greeted them at the door. 'Do come in, boys and gels,' she boomed in a voice loud enough to awaken the dead. 'I'm Dorothy Bassett-Wycliffe, but that's a bit of a mouthful so you may call me Mrs B.' She turned to a man who was standing behind her. 'And this is my husband, Reggie, who likes to be called "Skipper" because that's what everyone called him when he flew Lancaster Bombers.'

Skipper, who walked with a stick, was a thin man who only came up to his wife's shoulders. He stepped forward out of the shadows, and the children gasped when they saw the burn scars on his face.

There were angry-looking red patches of shrivelled skin above his eyes where his eyebrows should have been, and the top of his head looked like orange crepe paper. He had a magnificent handlebar moustache that he kept twisting with his fingers in order to make the ends stand out. 'Jolly good show,' he said, smiling at everyone as they all trooped over the doorstep.

Billy couldn't contain himself. 'How, did your face get burned, Skipper?' he said.

Jess prodded him with her elbow. '*Billy.*'

Skipper held up one shrivelled hand. 'It's all right, young lady,' he said. 'I'm used to people asking me that question. Sit you down and I'll tell you.'

The Woodlarks sat on the stairs to listen to Skipper's tale. 'I was Captain of a Lancaster bomber that got hit by a German fighter while on a raid over Germany,' he began. 'I managed, with my crew, to limp towards home on three engines, but then just before we crossed the English coastline, another engine cut out. I thought we were going to ditch into the sea but we battled on with only two engines, and were in sight of our base when something went wrong. The plane suddenly lost power and, without warning, nosedived onto the runway where it burst into flames.' Skipper, his face white, paused, and a worried Billy began to wish he'd not asked the old man about his face. 'I don't remember much after that,' Skipper went on. 'When I came to, I was in hospital, my head and hands covered in bandages and in a great deal of pain. I was one of the lucky ones

159

though. The rescue team reached me first and managed to drag me away from the inferno, but I lost all six of the other crew members.'

The children were silent.

'Well, that's it,' Mrs B boomed, wiping her eyes, and making them all jump. She turned to Skipper. 'Would you like to deal with the lemonade, please?' she said. 'Everything's ready in the kitchen.'

Skipper disappeared.

Mrs B led them into a room where, on a long table, a display of food such as none of the children had seen in a long time, made Billy's mouth water. There were sandwiches, pork pies, sausage rolls, bowls of pickled onions and tomatoes, and plates of iced buns and fancy cakes. She waved a hand in the direction of the table. 'Help yourselves,' she said, 'and try not to make too many crumbs on my best carpet.'

They all dived in, piling their plates as high as they could. Billy bit into a cheese and pickle sandwich. 'Mmm,' he said to Jess, 'I wonder where they got all this food from.'

'It's not your business,' she replied, tucking into a sausage roll. 'And you shouldn't have asked Skipper about his face, either.'

'He didn't mind.'

'No, but everyone else did. Mrs B looked really annoyed, and you made her cry.'

Billy turned and spoke to Danny. 'Did *you* know what had happened to your uncle?' he asked.

'Of course I did. He's a very brave man. He flew on loads of raids over Germany, and won the

DFC for his part in the Dambuster's raid. Then he went and pranged his Lancaster, and that was the end for him in the Air Force.'

'Blimey!'

'Now then, children,' Mrs B said from her arm chair, once the food had been demolished and the Woodlarks had settled themselves in a circle around her on the carpet, 'the tea is a reward for all the good work you've done in raising money for the war effort. Skipper and I thought you deserved a little treat.'

'Thank you,' they all said in turn.

'Are we going to do anything else?' Billy asked. 'For the war effort, I mean.'

'Well, we can have the village hall on 11th December, and I thought we'd hold a Rummage sale,' Mrs B said. 'The money we raise will be given to those villagers who have lost someone in the war, like Mrs Bunn, and poor Mrs McKenzie whose husband died in a raid over Portsmouth and left her with four children. And there are also one or two others that I know of.'

Jess nudged Billy. 'That's Dorothy McKenzie's dad. *You know* – the one I told you about,' she whispered.

'Yeah.' Billy wasn't sure about giving money to Mrs Bunn though. She'd probably spend it all on George.

Mrs B stood up and glanced at the clock on the mantelpiece. 'I'll book the hall, and leave it to you boys and gels to collect some bits and pieces to sell,'

161

she said. 'But now I think it's time you all went home. It's terribly dark out there.'

As they left the grounds of the house and began to walk along the blacked-out main road, the wail of the air raid siren echoed across the village. Billy's stomach turned over and he started to run.

'Don't be daft,' Sam called after him. 'The German aeroplanes don't come over this far.'

Billy stopped. 'What's *that* then?' he said, pointing to the sky. The drone of a single aircraft brought them all to a stop, and they looked up. Silhouetted against the light of a full moon, the aeroplane, it's engines making a sort of clanking noise, struggled to stay airborne. 'It's in trouble,' Billy shouted. 'Run for it!'

They ran. Along the road, through a hole in the hedge and across a field, while the troubled aircraft bore down upon them. Fear gripped Billy as he remembered the machine-gunning, and the air raid that had killed his friend. He thought his heart would burst out of his chest when suddenly the aircraft's engines stopped and everything went quiet. They all flung themselves down onto the frost-covered grass, clapping their hands over their ears. Billy didn't know what had happened to Jess. 'Jess, Jess, where are you?' he called out.

'It's all right, Billy, I'm over here,' she shouted. 'I'm with Danny.'

They lay there for a few minutes and then they heard the aircraft's engines splutter back into life. Billy couldn't resist lifting his head to have a look.

By the light of the moon, he saw it hover in the air like a giant blackbird, and then disappear from view as it plunged earthwards. The ground shook as, somewhere in the distance, the aircraft exploded and a ball of flame soared into the sky.

Billy couldn't stop shaking. 'I wonder where it crashed,' he said, as they all stood up and brushed the frost from their clothes. 'Come on, Jess, let's get home.'

A report in the Evening News the following day, said that a stray German Aeroplane had crashed into a hillside, several miles' north of the village of Horndean. As far as it was possible to tell, there were no civilian casualties but none of the crew had survived.

Chapter Twenty-Two

The Rummage sale

At the Christmas Rummage Sale, Billy found himself in charge of the bookstall. He and the other Woodlarks had collected so much stuff that there was hardly room for it all. The villagers had generously donated ornaments, old books, toys, strings of beads, and unwanted clothes, and Mrs B could hardly believe her eyes when she arrived to help set up the tables that morning.

'Well *done*,' she exclaimed. 'What a grand effort. If we only sell half this lot, there'll be enough money to give a few families a happy Christmas.'

Billy had persuaded Perizada to come along and take charge of one of the bric-a-brac tables. She had donated some of her bottles of flower water, a few bunches of dried lavender and an assortment of strings of beads she had made from papier mache. The sale began at nine o'clock, and an hour later, she had sold everything on her table.

'I'll come and help you,' she called over to Billy, whose books were selling fast.

'Thanks, Perizada.' He held up a copy of Arthur Ransome's Swallows and Amazons. 'I'm goin' to ask my mum if I can buy this,' he said. 'My class were reading it jus' before I came to Horndean an' I never finished it.'

Perizada gave a big sigh. 'I do wish I could read, Billy,' she said.

'I could teach you,' he offered.

She laughed. 'Thank you, Billy but I think I've left it too late now. B'sides, it won't be long before you go back to live in Portsmouth, and then what'll I do?'

Billy hadn't thought of that. 'I want to go to the lavvy,' he said, presently. 'Could you mind the table for me please?'

'Of course I will.'

When he came back, he found Perizada in a panic. 'I'm sorry, Billy,' she said, 'but someone's bought that book you wanted. He picked it up and put the money down on the table before I could stop him.'

'Oh, *no*.' Billy could have cried with disappointment, and then he saw Perizada's face. 'Never mind,' he said. 'I'll find another one somewhere. It doesn't matter. *Honest*.' They sold a few more books and then it went quiet for a bit. 'You had lots of people round your table,' he said. 'D'you think the villagers like you better now than they did once upon a time, Perizada?'

'Yes, Billy, I think they do, and it's really because of you.'

'Me?'

'Yes. Ever since I told fortunes at your garden fete, they've been much kinder to me. And I suspect they all enjoyed that little - er – *thing* with Mrs Baggit's hat.'

Billy laughed. 'You really *did* make that wind blow up, didn't you?'

Perizada's green eyes twinkled. 'If you say so, Billy,' she said. 'And poor old Mrs Baggit hasn't spoken to me since. Now, how's that arm of yours?'

'It still hurts a bit, but Doctor Bainbridge said I could leave the sling off now.'

'Billy Parkin,' she said, 'You're always in some pickle or other.'

'Pickle?'

'Yes. In trouble or in a scrape.'

'That's what my mum said the other day.'

'Well, she's right.'

They both laughed aloud, which attracted the attention of Mrs B, who came over to see what was going on. She looked at Perizada's empty table and then at the few books left on Billy's. Apart from the Woodlarks and a few helpers, the hall was now empty. 'This has been *most* successful,' she boomed. 'Skipper is, as I speak, counting the takings, so if you would let him have yours, he can tell us all how much money we've made.'

'Eight pounds, seven shillings and tuppence-farthing,' Skipper announced, fifteen minutes' later, when he'd checked the piles of coins lined up in front of him. 'That's absolutely *wizard,* everyone. Jolly good show. Well done.'

'I propose,' Mrs B said when the cheers and clapping had died down, 'that we look at the list of those villagers who are in greatest need this Christmas, and divide the money between them. All those in favour, please raise your hands.'

Everyone agreed and the job of clearing the hall began.

Later, Jess went off to find their mother who had gone to work in the café for the morning, taking Shirley with her, and Billy walked home with Perizada.

'Would you like a drink of lemonade?' Perizada asked as they reached the end of Woodsmoke Lane.

'Yes, please.'

As they turned into Potter's Lane, they saw Mrs Baggit leaning over her gate. 'You didn't come to our sale this morning, Mrs Baggit,' Billy said, watching her chins wobble all over the place as she shook her head.

'Not likely,' she replied, glaring at Perizada. 'I had enough of *her* jiggery pokery the last time, thanks very much.' She turned away and waddled up the path to her front door.

'She'll never forgive me for that,' Perizada said, with a wicked smile.

Billy settled down by the fire with his glass of home made lemonade while Perizada fed her cats. Over the fire, the cauldron bubbled away with something that smelled like the aniseed balls he used to love before sweets went on ration.

'It's Fennel,' she told him a bit later, 'For babbies when they have the wind.'

Billy was a bit puzzled. 'Who d'you sell it to?' he asked.

'Ah. That be my good friend, Doctor Bainbridge. He buys it from me. In fact, if it weren't for him, I'd be in the workhouse by now. And before you ask, Billy, the workhouse is where you go when you've got no money to live on.'

'I know,' he said. 'At school, I'm writing about the Victorians, an' lots of people went to the workhouse in them days.'

Perizada stared into the distance. 'Not very nice places,' she said, as if remembering something from the past. 'Anyway, Billy, I have something to tell you. Can you keep a secret?'

'I think so,' he said.

'Let me get you some more lemonade first.' She went into the kitchen and refilled his glass.

'What's this secret, then?' he asked, when she came back. 'An mustn't I tell *anyone*? Not even my mum?'

'*No one*, Billy, and unless you promise, I won't tell you.'

'All right. I promise.'

She left her seat, wandered over to the window and stared out into the garden. 'I'm getting married,' she said.

Billy choked on his lemonade. 'How can you get married, you 'aven't got a boy-friend, an' you're too old?'

'That's very rude, Billy,' Perizada said. 'And I do have a friend – a very good friend, in fact, who wants to marry me. I've known him since I were a little girl in St. Ives, and that's where he lives now. He's an artist.'

'Sorry,' Billy said. 'I thought you had to be young to get married. What's his name?'

'Thomas Lee. But I've always called him Tommo.'

'Is he Romany, like you?'

Perizada laughed. 'Oh, yes, Billy,' she said. 'It wouldn't do for me to marry a Gorgio. My old granny, if she were alive, would have forty fits if I did.'

'When's the wedding goin' to be?'

'In the spring. But I don't want anyone to know just yet, so don't forget your promise, will you?'

'No, I won't.' Billy finished his drink. 'Will you move away from here?' he asked.

'I daresay Tommo and I will live at St. Ives. He has a cottage there.'

Billy stared into his empty glass. 'I s'pose,' he said, 'that you won't come back to Horndean, *ever* again?'

'I shouldn't think so, Billy. But,' she went on, 'you'll be going back to Portsmouth next year I suspect. And once this rotten war's over, you'll be able to come to Cornwall for a holiday.'

Billy cheered up at that. 'Will you have any children?' he asked.

Perizada's face turned a deep red. 'Billy Parkin,' she said, 'you ask too many questions, and one of these days it'll get you into trouble.'

'I like to know about things,' he said.

'Well, you're not going to know about *this* thing,' she said. 'Now, I think it's time you went home.'

Billy stood up. 'Yeah, my mum'll be home from the café an' she'll wonder where I've got to. Thanks for the lemonade, Perizada.'

'Now just remember your promise not to say anything,' she said, as she showed him out. 'Not even to your *mum*.'

Chapter Twenty-Three

Christmas

On Christmas Eve, Billy's father came home from work early and brought with him two dead rabbits. 'There we are,' he said, dumping the two stiff little bodies on the kitchen table, 'Christmas dinner.'

Two pairs of glassy eyes stared up at Billy and he turned his face away. 'Where did you get them, Dad?' he said, feeling just a bit sick.

'Never you mind. Just think yourself lucky that your mother will have something to put on the table tomorrow. There's nothing to be had in the shops.'

'D'you cook them with their fur on?' Shirley asked, and everyone laughed.

'Don't be so daft,' Billy said. 'Mum's goin' to skin them first, aren't you, Mum?'

'No, Billy. *You* are going to skin them for me.'

'I am *not*.'

'Your mother's just teasing,' his father said. 'I'll do the skinning, and then we can cure the fur and make some mittens.'

'That's *horrible*,' Billy said, and went into his bedroom, away from the staring eyes of the two animals.

That night, Billy took a long time to get to sleep, what with thinking about the rabbits, and wondering what presents he'd find in the pillow case at the foot of his bed. It must have been very early the next morning when he woke and heard Jess and

Shirley giggling in their bedroom. He decided to get up and see what they were doing. They had already opened their presents and he went back into his bedroom to get his. A Biggles book, an orange, a handful of nuts and a parcel all wrapped up in sparkly paper. He tore it open and his eyes popped. An Arthur Ransome, Swallows and Amazons book – the one Perizada had said she'd sold at the Rummage sale. Inside the front cover, she'd written:

"Sorry I had to tell you a fib. With best wishes from your friend, Perizada".

'Look what Perizada's given me,' he said, holding it up for them to see.

'And she's given Shirley and me some of those beads she makes,' Jess said, showing him the brightly coloured necklace she'd found among the orange and nuts in her pillow case. 'And I've got another Angela Brazil book, "The Mystery of the Moated Grange".

Billy burst out laughing. 'Dunno how you can read all that rubbish,' he said.

'Shut up, *you.*'

'What did *you* get?' he asked Shirley.

'An orange, some nuts and some chocolate pennies,' she said. 'And a dolly. Look.' She held up a china doll dressed in knitted clothes.

'Blimey, I wonder where mum got that from,' Billy said.

'Some lady in the village,' Jess said. 'She didn't have any children left at home, and had some of their stuff for sale. That's where she bought your stupid Biggles book from, too.'

'All right, know-all,' Billy said.

'I'm only *saying*.'

A head appeared round the door. 'Arguing on Christmas Day?' their mother asked.

'No, Mum,' Billy and Jess said together.

'Well, now that you've opened everything, and woken your father and me up, you can just go back to bed until it's time for breakfast. It's only five o'clock.'

Billy slept after that, and didn't wake up until his mother shook him and told him that breakfast was ready.

'I think, Billy,' she said, once breakfast was over, 'that when Perizada comes back, you should all go round and thank her for the presents she gave you.'

Billy was puzzled. 'Come back?' he said. 'Has she gone away then?'

'Yes. When she brought your presents round last week she told me she would be going to Cornwall for Christmas, to see a friend.'

'Oh, I know who ...', Billy almost gave away Perizada's secret. 'She didn't tell *me*,' he said.

'No, she'd only just made up her mind to go, and I forgot to tell you.'

'It's a long way from here, isn't it?'

'Yes.'

'When will she be back?' Billy wanted to know.

'The day after tomorrow. That's if she can get a train.'

Billy wandered off to the living room and looked out of the window at the cold, crisp morning. 'I'm goin' for a walk,' he shouted to his mother. 'Won't be long.'

She put her head round the door. 'Wrap yourself up. It's perishing cold out there.'

He put on his thick coat, pulled his socks up over his knees and, with a scarf wrapped around his neck, set off down the lane. His mother was right. The cold air caught at his throat and made him cough, and he could see his own breath as it formed a cloud of steam in front of his face. He shivered and was just about to turn back when he caught sight of George walking towards him with a dog on the end of a lead.

'Whose dog is that?' Billy said as they drew level.

'Mine. My mum bought it for me for Christmas. An old lady down the village gave her some money.'

Billy bent down to pat the pure white fur. 'What make is he?' he said.

'You mean what *breed*,' George said, knowledgeably.

'All right. What *breed*?'

'He's a Highland Terrier, an' I've called him Dougal,' George said.

'That's a funny name for a dog.'

'So what.'

'All right, keep your hair on.' Billy let Dougal lick his hand. The dog put its head on one side and looked at him from its black, boot-button eyes. 'I wish my mum would let me have a dog,' he said. 'All we've got is Shirley's mangy cat, an' I hate that.'

'D'you want to come for a walk with us?' George offered. 'I'll let you hold the lead if you like.'

This new friendliness from George surprised Billy. 'Yeah, all right,' he said.

George handed him the lead. 'He's only a puppy so don't pull on it, else you'll hurt his neck.'

They walked around the woods for a bit and then sat down on a log. Dougal sniffed around, and then came and sat at Billy's feet. 'He likes you,' George said.

Billy ran his fingers through Dougal's fur. 'That's 'cos I like dogs. Dogs know if you like them or not,' he said.

'If you've never bin allowed to 'ave a dog, how come you know so much about them?'

'My Grandma Parkin used to have one. She's dead now.'

'Who is? Your Grandma or the dog?'

Billy laughed. 'Both of them,' he said.

They sat in silence for a few minutes. Billy went on tickling Dougal and George stared into space and bit his nails. 'I'm havin' a new dad,' he said presently.

'A new dad?'

'Yep. He's a sailor, like my old dad.'

'What's he like?' Billy asked.

George's eyes filled with tears. 'I don't like 'im,' he said. 'He squeezes my arm when my mum's not looking. An' he didn't want her to buy me a dog. An' I want my own dad back.'

'Is this new dad goin' to marry your mum?'

George shrugged. 'I dunno,' he said. 'I 'spect so. If he does, I think they're goin' t'move to Portsmouth.'

Billy laughed. 'I'll be able to call *you* a Pompey Fleabag then, won't I,' he said.

'Yeah, I s'ppose so. Any case, if they get married I'm goin' to run away.'

'Don't be daft,' Billy said, feeling sorry for his old enemy. 'The police will bring you back an' then you'll be in trouble.'

George stood up. 'Yeah, an' I'll be trouble if I don't get home for my dinner,' he said, taking Dougal's lead. 'Don't tell anyone about my new dad, will you? My mum wants it kept a secret for now.'

'I won't.' Billy wondered how many more secrets he would have to keep. First Perizada, and now George's mum. 'I tell you what,' he said, 'why don't we be friends? I could help you with Dougal – take him for walks an' that.'

George's face lit up. 'All right,' he said. 'An' it would be like havin' your own dog. Well, *almost.*'

'Yeah. That'd be wizard,' Billy said. 'Call for me tomorrow morning an' I'll come out with you.'

The two boys parted company and as Billy walked home, he shoved his hands in his pockets, and whistled a tune. Helping with someone else's dog wasn't quite the same as having your own, but it was better than nothing. All the same, he wondered how long he and George would be able to remain friends.

'George Bunn's got a dog,' he said to his mother as he went indoors. 'A Highland Terrier, an' I'm goin' to help him take it for walks an' that.'

She looked surprised. 'Well, it's nice that you two are making friends, I suppose,' she said. 'But don't go asking me if you can have a dog, because you can't.'

'I bet if I asked for a rotten old cat, you'd let me,' Billy said.

'That'll be enough from you. I'm busy getting dinner so go and read your new book or something.'

Billy picked at the portion of rabbit on his plate. In his mind, he could still see the two pairs of glassy eyes staring up at him. 'I can't eat this,' he said, pushing his plate away.

'You'll eat it or there's no pudding,' his mother said.

His father pulled Billy's discarded plate across the table. 'I'll finish it off,' he said. 'And you, Billy, can eat up the greens and carrots. Your mother's worked hard to give us a Christmas dinner, and you should be thankful.'

'*Yes*, Dad.'

Billy ate up the greens, which he hated, and the carrots, which he didn't mind too much. He didn't want to miss out on the Christmas pudding his mother had made. She'd saved enough dried fruit, whenever she could get it, and made everyone take saccharin instead of sugar in their tea. To make the pudding dark, she'd used cold tea, and dried instead of fresh egg. When she served it up, it didn't look any different from those she'd made before the war. Billy smacked his lips together.

'No custard, I'm afraid,' she said. 'But I've taken the cream off the top of three pints of milk, and you can have that if you like.'

'We used to have crackers on the table before the war,' Billy said, as he scraped the last of the pudding from his dish.

'We had lots of things before the war,' his father replied, 'and will do again, once it's all over. In the meantime, you can all give your mother a hand to clear up while I go outside for a breath of fresh air.'

Billy helped clear the table. 'Why don't you go and talk to your dad?' his mother said, after he'd bumped into her and the knives and forks slid off the plates onto the floor. 'There's not room for all of us in this kitchen.'

He went outside. 'I wish mum would let me have a dog,' he said. 'Why won't she, Dad?'

'Because she doesn't like dogs, and she'd have to do most of the looking after while you're at school. Feed it, walk it and clean up after it. It wouldn't be right.'

'Shirley's got a cat.'

Billy's father gave him a dark look. 'That's different,' he said. 'Cats look after themselves. I don't know how many more times I have to tell you why you can't have a dog, Billy. Now, for goodness sake stop going on about it. You can't have one and that's that, and I don't want to hear any more about it.'

Billy went back indoors, walked past his mother without a word, and into his bedroom. There, curled up on his bed, and fast asleep was the cat, Raffles. 'Come an' get your mangy cat off my bed,' he yelled at Shirley, who was sitting by the fire playing with her doll.

'No,' she said. 'He's not hurting anything.'

'*Right*.' Billy said. He grabbed Raffles by the scruff of the neck, marched into the living room and dropped him into Shirley's lap. 'Keep this fleabag out've my bedroom, else I'll take him down the village an' get rid of him.'

Their mother appeared in the doorway. 'Go to your bedroom, Billy, and don't come out again until teatime. I've just about had enough of you and your nonsense.'

'It's Christmas Day,' he whined.

'All the more reason why you should behave yourself,' she said.

Billy went, slamming the door behind him and lay on his bed, wondering how a day that had started so well could end up with him sent to his room. And all because of a *cat*. 'I've a good mind to take it down the village and lose it,' he said aloud to himself.

He picked up his Arthur Ransome book and began to read but within minutes, his eyelids began to droop and he fell asleep. When he woke up, it was dark and he could hear his mother clattering around in the kitchen. He rubbed the sleepy dust from his eyes and went out to see what she was doing.

'Getting tea,' she said, when he asked. 'It's almost six o'clock, Billy.' She didn't mention the cat, and the rest of Christmas Day passed without any argument or telling off.

'I'm goin' to meet George tomorrow morning,' Billy said, before he went to bed. 'We're takin' his dog for a walk.'

Shirley opened her mouth to say something but their mother silenced her with a look.

'That's good, Billy,' she said, smiling at him for the first time that day.

Chapter Twenty-Four

A New Friendship

On Boxing Day morning, Billy pressed his nose up against the window. 'I wish it would snow,' he said to his mother. So far this winter, there hadn't been any, apart from a few flurries on Christmas Eve. 'I want to see the trees all covered in white, and have a game of snowballs with my friends.'

'We can do without any of that,' she replied. 'It might look nice, but I can just imagine what the lane would be like when it thawed.'

'Aw, Mum.'

'I thought you were going out with George and his dog this afternoon.'

'Yeah, I am.'

She gave a deep sigh. 'I do wish you would say *yes,* instead of *yeah,* Billy.'

'*Yes*, Mum.'

After dinner, he fetched his coat and pulled on his Wellington boots. 'I'm goin' now, Mum,' he called through to the kitchen.

'All right, but make sure you're back before dark.'

As he walked down the lane, he saw George coming towards him with Dougal on a lead. 'Where shall we go?' Billy asked.

'I know a good place where you can see for miles,' George said. 'Follow me.'

They went down the side of Jethro Quirk's shack, and Billy pointed to the closed curtains at the windows. 'I haven't seen the old man lately,' he said. 'I wonder if he's all right.'

'He's dead,' George said. 'Took away on Christmas Eve, my mum said.'

'What for?'

'I dunno. I think he had a bad heart or somethin'.'

As they passed Danny's cottage, he came out of his front door clutching a large box under his arm.

'What've you got there?' Billy asked, knowing that it was bound to be something expensive Danny had had for Christmas. He always had the best of everything, even though there was a war on.

'It's a Hornby train set,' Danny said, 'I'm just taking it round to show Sam.'

'Blimey. Where did you get it?

Danny looked down his nose at them. 'My father bought it,' he said. 'He knows a lot of people.'

'Yeah, I bet he does,' Billy said as he and George walked on.

'Why d'you want to be friends with me?' George asked presently, as they sat down on a log to rest their legs.

'Why not? You haven't got any friends, and mine got killed in an air raid.'

'You go to the Woodlarks though.'

Billy laughed out aloud. 'Yeah,' he said. 'An' who d'you think's in charge? Danny Palmer of course, an' I don't like him. He's too big for his boots.'

'Tell me about your friend getting killed,' George said.

Billy hadn't talked about Dave to anyone, but for some reason he found it easy to tell George everything. They must have sat there for half-an-hour, and even Dougal stopped pulling at his lead and sat quietly with his head on one side, listening as Billy told his story.

'Blimey!' George said when he had finished. 'Fancy all those boys gettin' killed.'

'*And* girls,' Billy reminded him. He jumped to his feet. 'Anyway,' he said, 'we'd better take Dougal for his walk. Could I hold the lead?'

'Yep.'

They went through a part of the woods where Billy hadn't been before, and when they came out on the other side, he cried out in surprise. Spread out before them, a patchwork of villages, fields, valleys and hills stretched as far as the eye could see. 'Where are we?' he asked George, 'an' what's that place down there?'

'That's Clanfield,' George said. 'A German aeroplane crashed there the other day.'

'I know,' Billy said. 'I saw it come down.'

'An' see that road right over there?' George pointed to where a road split the countryside in two. 'That goes to London. An' years an' years ago, Highwaymen rode their hosses along there an' robbed all the rich people who were ridin' by in their carriages.'

'Get away,' Billy said, amazed at how much George seemed to know about things.

'It's true. That big hill you can see is Butser, an' the Highwaymen used to lie in wait among the trees at the bottom an' then pounce, just like Dick Turpin in the story.'

'An' what's at the other side of the hill?' Billy asked.

'That's Petersfield. My grandma used to live there an' my mum used to take me to see her. Then grandma died an' we didn't go any more.'

'Is it a big town, then?'

'No. But it's got a nice lake, an' sometimes a cattle market. D'you want to see that road where the Highwaymen went?' George said.

Billy looked up at the sky. It looked as if it might rain at any minute but he really wanted to see the road George was on about. He wound Dougal's lead tightly around his hand. 'Let's go,' he said.

They were standing on an embankment and the only way down was to slide sideways. With Dougal leaping about and barking his head off with all the excitement, they managed to reach a narrow lane leading to a field full of cows. 'Through here,' George said, opening a five-bar gate.

The animals stopped chewing the grass and swung their heads round to see what was going on. 'I'm not goin' in there,' Billy said. 'Look at their *eyes.*'

George carried on. 'Oh, don't be so daft. They won't hurt you if you just walk slowly.'

Billy crept behind George, watching the cows from the corner of his eye, until they came to a stile leading into an empty field. They climbed over.

'Now run,' George said. 'If farmer Franklin catches us, we'll be in trouble.'

They ran as fast as they could, and then Billy caught his foot in a rut and went sprawling in the wet grass.

'Oi, *you* there.' The farmer's voice echoed from across the field.

'Get up,' George said. 'C'mon.'

Billy scrambled to his feet. He handed Dougal's lead to George. 'I've twisted me ankle,' he said. 'You go on an' I'll catch you up.'

'No. It's too late. Ole Franklin's caught us.'

Billy looked up. Farmer Franklin was just a few yards' away. 'Git off my land, you young varmints or I'll have the police to you.'

'We weren't doin' anythin', Mister Franklin,' George said, in his best voice. 'I were just goin' to show my friend the road to London, that's all.'

The farmer relented. 'All right,' he said. 'But don't let me catch you here again. I'm getting' fed up with any ole Tom, Dick or Harry using my land as a short cut.'

'Yes, Mister Franklin.'

By this time, Billy was feeling cold, wet and tired, and he had mud all over his trousers. *And* it was beginning to get dark. His mother would give him what-for when he got home. 'Let's go home now,' he said to George, hoping that he would want to do the same.

'You wanted to see the road, an' we're nearly there,' George said. 'Follow me.'

Not many minutes' later, they came to the London Road. 'It's just the same as any other old road,' Billy complained, as he looked up and down the very ordinary strip of grey tarmac, which was hardly visible in the fading light.

'Yeah, but it wasn't like this in the olden days, and you said you wanted to see it.'

'All right, but I want to go home now.'

Going back wasn't as easy. They had to creep along the edge of farmer Franklin's field this time so that they couldn't be seen, and when George climbed the stile into the field of cows, Billy refused to follow him. 'I'm not going to walk past *them* again,' he said. 'It's nearly dark, and we'll be treadin' in cows droppings.'

George climbed back again. 'I s'ppose you're right,' he said. 'We'll just have to find some other way.'

By this time, it was dark and raining hard; cold, sleety stuff that stung their faces and legs. They stumbled along, hoping to find the way back to the woods from where they'd come, but with the moon behind the clouds and everywhere blacked out, they could see nothing at all. 'We're lost,' Billy said presently, frightened now of what would happen if they couldn't find their way out of here. In his imagination, he could see bold headlines on the front of the Evening News – "*Two young boys found dead on farmland at Horndean, after getting lost in the blackout*". *Billy Parkin and George Bunn were found this morning huddled together in the corner of a field ....*".

'Look over there.' George's voice brought Billy back to the present. 'There's someone with a torch movin' about.' The sound of a shotgun going off made them jump, and Dougal bark. 'Poachers,' he went on, 'out shootin' rabbits.'

Billy thought briefly of two pairs of glassy eyes looking up at him from the kitchen table. It had stopped raining and he looked up at the sky as a full moon appeared from behind the clouds. 'Look,' he said, pointing to a hole in the hedge, 'through there.'

They scrambled through the gap and landed in a ditch on the other side. 'My mum'll skin me alive when she sees all this mess on my clothes,' Billy said, shaking the water from his coat as best he could.

'You're lucky if you only get a tellin' off. *Mine'll* give me a good hiding.'

They crept forward to where the poacher was stringing two dead rabbits together.

'What're you doin', mister?' Billy said.

The startled man dropped his ill-gotten gains, and swung round, blinding the two boys with the light from his torch. 'What the devil are *you* doing spying on me?' he wanted to know.

Billy kept his eye on the shotgun, which the man had tucked under his arm. 'We're not spyin', mister,' he said. 'We're lost.'

'Whereabouts d'you live?'

'Woodsmoke Lane.'

'Go straight on down this path and you'll come to it.' The man jabbed a finger into Billy's chest. 'And don't you say anything about seeing me in here shooting rabbits or I'll have your guts for garters. And you too,' he said to George.

The boys fled. 'Did you know him?' Billy asked George as they came out of the woods into Woodsmoke Lane.

'Yeah. He lives in the village, on his own. Everyone says he's mad.'

'Oh, well,' Billy said, glad to be home. ' I'm not goin' to say anything.'

'Nor me,' George agreed. 'See you tomorrow?

Billy ruffled Dougal's head. 'Yep,' he said. 'That's if I'm allowed out.'

They parted company and Billy went down the side of Railway Cottage, hoping to sneak in the back door without his mother seeing him. He pushed open the door and stood on the mat inside, dripping water, mud and wet leaves all over the floor. She was standing by the cooker watching him.

'Where have you been?' she said, in a voice Billy knew meant trouble.

'For a walk. We got lost.'

'I'll give you "got lost",' she said. 'I told you to be home before dark. And just look at the state of you.'

'Sorry, Mum.'

'One of these days, you *will* be, Billy Parkin. Now get out of those wet things before you catch your death of cold. That's unless you already have.'

Later, as he sat up in bed drinking the hot cup of cocoa she'd brought in to him, he wondered if Mrs Bunn had given George the good hiding he'd expected. As he settled down under the covers, Billy thought about the days' events. Even though he'd felt a bit scared when they'd got lost, it had been fun, and George wasn't such a bad friend to have.

Chapter Twenty-Five

New Year 1944

When Billy woke up the following morning, his head ached and he had a strange feeling that he was floating around the bedroom. First, he felt hot, then cold and shivery and when he tried to call out to his mother, no sound came and his throat felt as if it were on fire. He pulled the blankets up over his chin and went back to sleep.

Some time later, when he next opened his eyes, he saw Doctor Bainbridge standing at the side of the bed. 'He has a very high temperature, Mrs Parkin,' he heard the doctor say. 'Keep him in bed for a few days.' He handed Billy's mother a bottle. 'Give him a tablespoonful of this three times' a day, and he'll soon be on the mend.'

'That's what comes of wandering around getting lost in the cold and wet,' she said to Billy after the doctor had left. She measured out a tablespoonful of the medicine into a cup. 'Now drink this and go back to sleep.'

Billy drifted in and out of sleep all night. Now and then, he opened his eyes but closed them again quickly when the room spun like a whirligig and he felt as if he would fall out of bed onto the floor. Once, from a long way away, he heard the voice of Dave Spiller calling out to him.

'I'm behind here, Billy,' Dave shouted. *'I can't get out. Come and find me.'*

But all that Billy could see was a pile of bricks as tall as a house, and after a minute or two, Dave's voice faded away. Billy must have called out because when he opened his eyes, his mother was standing at the side of the bed.

'You've had a bad dream, Billy,' she said, feeling his forehead with a cool hand. 'And you're still very hot.' She helped him to sit up, gave him some more medicine and a drink of water. 'Would you like me to stay for a while?'

'No thanks, Mum,' Billy said, in a croaky voice. 'I'll be all right now.'

He must have then fallen into a deep sleep, for when he woke up it was daylight and he could hear everyone moving about in the cottage. A head appeared round the door. 'Hello,' Jess said, 'how are you?'

'A bit better I think,' Billy said. If he didn't move his head too quickly, he didn't feel dizzy, but his throat was still dry and sore. 'Could you get me a drink, please?'

'I'll ask mum, only she told Shirley and me not to come in here in case we caught something.'

'Thanks,' Billy said. Another head came round the door.

'Hello.' This time it was Shirley. 'Mummy says you're ill. Are you going to die?' she asked.

Billy rolled his eyes, clutched first at his chest and then at his forehead. 'I expect so,' he said, enjoying all the attention he was getting.

'Well, if you do, please can I have your bedroom?'

'I s'pose so. Will you miss me when I'm gone?'

Tears welled up in Shirley's eyes and ran down her face. She wiped her nose in her sleeve.

'I don't really want you to die,' she said, 'but I want a room all to myself.'

'I'll see what I can do,' Billy said. 'What's the time?'

'I don't know, but we've had our breakfast and mummy's getting ready to go out.'

'Oh.' All this talking was making Billy's throat worse, and he was glad to see his mother appear with a glass of water.

'What's been going on here?' she asked. 'Why is Shirley crying?'

'Billy says he's going to die,' Shirley said.

Doris Parkin gave Billy one of her disapproving looks. 'We'll have none of that kind of talk, Billy Parkin,' she said. 'Now, take your medicine, drink this water and stop making your sister cry.'

'I'm hungry,' Billy said. 'Could I have something to eat?'

'There's porridge.'

'Ugh!'

'Well, it'll have to do for now. There's nothing to be had in the shops until they get their deliveries.'

Billy ate his porridge. He tried to remember what day of the week it was. He'd gone for a walk with George on Boxing day; the day after that his father had gone back to work and he, Billy, had been

taken ill, so it must be the 28th December. He
wondered if George was all right.

'Has George Bunn been round to see me?' he
asked his mother when she came back to tidy up his
bed.

'No. I expect he's been ill too,' she said. 'The
pair of you haven't got the sense you were born
with.'

'If he comes, could you let him come in an'
see me?'

Doris Parkin fussed around straightening the
bedcovers. 'As long as he doesn't have the dog with
him,' she said. 'Doctor Bainbridge is calling in later
on to see how you are, and I'm sending Jess and
Shirley to thank your friend, Perizada, for her
Christmas presents.'

'Mum?'

'Yes?'

'I'm not really goin' to die, am I?'

She laughed. 'There's an old saying, Billy, that
only the good die young. And if that's the case, I
should think *you'll* live to be one-hundred. Of
course, you're not going to die. Now settle down
before Doctor Bainbridge comes.'

'Another day or two in bed and you'll be able
to get up and about,' the doctor said when later, he
looked in to see Billy.

'Is that medicine one of Perizada's potions?'
Billy asked.

The doctor shook his head. 'I'm afraid you
needed something a bit stronger this time,' he said,

'but there's no harm in asking her for some of her tonic, once you're feeling better.'

When the doctor had gone, Billy picked up his Arthur Ransome book and began to read but it was all too much of an effort. His eyelids felt heavy, all he wanted to do was go back to sleep. Just before he dropped off, he wondered if he'd ever feel well again.

Jess brought a note and an orange for Billy from Perizada. He sniffed at the fruit, dug his fingernails into the skin and began to peel it, the smell making his mouth water. He couldn't remember the last time he'd had an orange. He looked up at Jess and Shirley, who were watching him with open mouths, and offered them a segment each. 'Only one,' he said. 'The rest is for me 'cos I've been ill.'

Jess handed him an envelope that smelled of Perizada's cooking pot. 'She says she hopes you'll soon be better,' she said.

He opened the letter.

"Dear Billy,' he read
Sorry to hear you are poorly and hope you'll soon be better. This orange will do you good but don't ask where it came from. Come and see me when you are well again as I want to talk to you about something.'
Kind regards
Your friend, Perizada"

'Did she really write this?' Billy asked.

'Yes,' Jess said. 'Why?'

'Well, she can't read, so how can she do this joined-up writing, *and* spell all the words properly?'

'I don't know, but she wrote it while we were there. We saw her do it. What does she say?'

'Mind your own business, nosey Parker,' Billy said, shoving the letter under his pillow.

Two days later, he felt well enough to get up. 'Could I down the lane and see George?' he asked his mother

'You'll do no such thing,' she said. 'It's wet and cold out there and I want you fit to go back to school next week.'

'But I want to know what's happened to him.'

'I'm going shopping presently,' she said. 'I'll call in and find out.'

'Thanks, Mum.'

He curled up with his book in the armchair by the fire. Although he *did* feel better, his legs were all weak and wobbly, and he felt tired all the time. All the same, he was worried about George, and could hardly wait to find out why he hadn't called.

'George has not been allowed out,' she told him when she came back. 'His mother made him stay indoors all week and do jobs for her, to teach him a lesson. She's going to let him come and see you after dinner today.'

'Was his new dad there?' Billy said, without thinking.

'New dad?'

'Yeah. He's got a new dad but it's supposed to be a secret, an' I forgot.'

'I think you've got it all wrong, Billy,' she said. 'There was a man there but George's mum said he was her brother.'

'Oh. That makes him George's uncle then?'

'Yes.'

George turned up at two o'clock, looking paler and thinner than ever. 'Did you get into much trouble?' Billy asked. 'My mum says you weren't allowed out.'

'Yeah, that's right. It was *him* who said I had to stay indoors, not my mum.'

'Do you mean your uncle?'

'He's not my uncle. My mum only said that 'cos she doesn't want anyone to know I've got a new father.'

Billy changed the subject. 'How's Dougal?' he said.

'He's all right. My mum's been takin' him for walks. She went mad when she saw all that mud on his coat the other day.' George looked around the room. 'This is nice an' cosy, isn't it?'

'I s'pose so,' Billy agreed.

His mother appeared with two glasses of hot blackcurrant juice and some biscuits. 'Here you are,' she said, 'drink this up. It'll do you good.'

'I like your mum,' George said, when she'd gone back into the kitchen. 'She's nice.'

'She's all right,' Billy said, 'except that she *fusses*.'

George stayed for the rest of the afternoon. He and Billy played Snakes and Ladders and Ludo while Billy's mother took Jess and Shirley shopping. At half-past-four, George said he ought to go home.

'See you tomorrow, then?' Billy said.

'Yep. If I'm allowed, I'll call round after dinner.'

When George had gone, Billy curled up in his dad's armchair and fell asleep.

After breakfast the next day, Billy spent some time looking out of the window, wishing he could go out for a walk. 'It's not raining,' he said to his mother. 'Why can't I go?'

'Because,' she said, handing him a glass with his medicine in it, 'it's too cold. You don't want to catch pneumonia, do you?'

'What's pneumonia?'

'It's where your lungs get all bunged up and you can't breathe.'

'Yeah, but Jess and Shirley are going out.'

'Well, they haven't been ill. Now stop complaining and read your book.'

Billy picked up his Swallows and Amazons but found he couldn't concentrate on reading. Instead, he sat and thought about school. Every January, so he'd been told, one pupil from each local school had their name put forward for a competition to find the best historical essay – the prize, a book and your name engraved on a shield. He would love to have a go but it was up to the English teachers to choose who would enter, and Billy wouldn't stand a chance if old Skinter had anything to do with it.

Presently, the sound of voices caught his ear. He went to the window and peered out. Coming up the path, in a single line led by Jess and Shirley, were all the Woodlarks.

'Boots and shoes off, please,' he heard his mother say. She held the door open and they piled in, all talking at once.

'We've come bearing gifts,' Danny said, handing Billy a bar of Fry's Five Boys chocolate. 'Just like the Three Wise Men.' Everyone laughed, although Billy thought Danny was showing off as usual.

Billy had a Dandy comic from Sam, a Beano from Nancy, and two packets of sherbet dabs from Meg. 'Thanks,' Billy said. 'All my favourite things.'

They sat in a semi-circle on the floor around Billy's chair.

'Is that right you've made friends with George Bunn?' Danny asked.

'Who told you that?' Billy wanted to know.

'Ah, that would be telling. Is it true, then?'

If it hadn't been for the bar of Five Boys chocolate Danny had brought him, Billy would have said something rude and nasty. 'Yes, it is,' he said. 'He hasn't got any friends, an' I'm helping him with his new dog.'

'Oh.'

'An' I was goin' to ask him if he wanted to join the Woodlarks.' Billy hadn't really thought of any such thing but it was worth saying, just to see the look on Danny's face.

'Too late,' Danny said, pompously. 'I've decided to disband it.'

'Why?' Sam asked.

'Yes, *why?*' Meg put in.

For once, Danny was stuck for words. 'You're just saying that,' Billy said, 'so's you won't have to have George in it.'

'No I'm not. We've done all the fund-raising we can do, and there's no point in going on. Besides, I've got a lot of studying to do now.'

Nancy cut short Billy's retort. 'Let's change the subject,' she said. 'We came here to see Billy, not to have an argument.'

They talked about school, the end of the war, which they all thought was just around the corner, and what they planned to do when it was all over.

'We're goin' back to Pompey,' Billy said.

'And we're moving to Dorset with our dad's job,' Sam added.

'What about you, Meg?' Danny asked.

'Oh, we'll stay here I expect. My dad works in Waterlooville so there's no need for us to go anywhere.'

'And what are you goin' to do?' Billy asked Danny.

''I'm staying on at school, and then going to university to study politics,' he said.

'So, you're goin' to be our Prime Minister one day?'

'Probably.'

Everyone laughed. Trust Danny to be better than anyone else.

After they had all gone, Billy looked at the presents they'd brought him. Although he hadn't really liked being ill, he'd enjoyed all the fuss everyone had made of him. And he loved Five Boys milk chocolate. He decided to share it with George that afternoon but George didn't turn up.

'I 'spect he's been kept in again,' Billy said to his mother as he settled down to eat the whole bar of chocolate himself.

Chapter Twenty-Six

Back to School

As soon as his mother would let him go out, Billy went to see Perizada, to thank her for the orange and find out why she wanted to talk to him. He guessed it would be about the wedding.

'It's good to see you out and about again, Billy,' she said, as he sat down by the fire. 'And I was really pleased that your sisters came to see me.'

'What did Shirley do?' he asked. 'I mean ... did she scream or anythin'?'

'Why ever would she do that?'

'Well, she's always makin' a fuss about something.'

'She didn't scream *or* make a fuss.' Perizada brought two hot drinks over on a tray and sat opposite Billy. 'In fact, I want to ask your mother if she and Jess can be flower maidens at my wedding.'

'Are you goin' to have a proper Romany wedding?'

'No, Billy. Tommo wants it to be a quiet do, and he says we can have it here at Horndean, in that little chapel up on the main road. I shall like that, and it means you will be able to come.'

Billy laughed. 'That's good,' he said, 'as long as you don't want me to dress up in velvet trousers an' be a page boy. My Auntie Joan got married last year an' my two cousins had to do that. They looked stupid.'

'Don't worry; I won't be having any page boys.'

Billy sighed with relief. 'You didn't make any spelling mistakes in that note you sent me,' he said. 'How did you do that if you can't read or write?'

'Oh, but I *can* read and write, Billy,' she said. 'You see, Tommo isn't only an artist. He's a teacher of English and when I told him I couldn't read, he asked a good friend of his who lives just a mile or two away from here, to teach me. I've been having reading lessons for quite a while now. Since before you came here to live, in fact.'

'You didn't tell me.'

'That's because I didn't get on with it very well at first. The older you get, Billy, the harder it is to learn anything. But I'm doing nicely now, so my teacher, Harold Bridger, says.'

Billy studied Perizada for a minute. She was quite pretty really, especially when she smiled and her eyes sparkled. 'Well,' he said, 'If I were a bit older, I'd marry you myself.'

Her tinkling laugh echoed around the room. 'Billy Parkin,' she said, 'I don't think I've ever met such a cheeky young ruffian in all my life. Now, finish your drink.'

'D'you want me to ask my mum about Jess and Shirley?' he said, as she showed him to the door.

She shook her head. 'No, Billy. I'll come round and see her for myself. She'll want to know about their dresses, and all sorts of things.' She bent down and planted a kiss on the side of Billy's face. 'I'm so happy to be marrying Tommo,' she said.

School re-opened on the fourth of January, and Billy was glad to go back. Although he and George had taken Dougal out nearly every day, *and* made sure they were back before dark, Billy found the holiday dragged on for too long. Back in Portsmouth, he would have gone to see Tarzan or Roy Rogers at the Regal, had a game of football or a bit of a skylark in the park, but there was nothing like that here. Even though he liked living in the country, there wasn't much to do in the winter, and he was bored.

After the usual scramble for desks and seats, Billy's class settled down to the first English lesson of the new term. Horace Skinter called the register, his beady little eyes resting on each boy in turn, as he shouted out their name. He did this to stop anyone answering for a missing pupil who had decided to skip school for the day. Having satisfied himself that everything was in order, he put the register away in a cupboard, sat at his desk and faced the class.

Billy felt all eyes on him as Horace Skinter pointed a finger in his direction. 'You, Parkin,' he bellowed across the classroom, 'are to report to the headmaster's office this morning at play time.'

'Yes, sir,' Billy said, wondering what he'd done *this* time to upset the English teacher. School had only just re-opened after the Christmas holiday so it must have been something he'd done before it broke up. 'Why does he want to see me, sir?'

'It's not your place to ask questions, Parkin,' Horace Skinter said. 'You'll just do as you are told.'

'Yes, sir.'

At ten-fifteen, Billy tapped on the door of the Headmaster's office and went inside. James Armitage was at his desk, with Horace Skinter in a chair to his right. Billy's heart sank. He could feel his legs trembling, and a horrible churning up in his stomach of the breakfast his mother had made him eat that morning. If Horace Skinter was here, it must mean trouble.

The Headmaster gave Billy a wide smile and nodded towards the English teacher. 'Mister Skinter, here,' he began, 'tells me that you are one of his brightest pupils and that, for the past few months, you have regularly achieved top marks in English. He feels, and I agree, that you should enter this year's essay competition.'

Billy's eyebrows shot up in surprise. Old Skinter praising him? He couldn't believe his ears.

'Well, Parkin, you seem to have been struck dumb. What do you say?'

'Thank you, sir … *and* Mister Skinter.'

Horace Skinter smiled, showing a perfect set of false teeth that were too big for his mouth. 'You may choose your own subject,' he said, 'and you have two weeks in which to complete your essay. The results and presentation will be held on the twenty-seventh of January.'

'That's my birthday, sir,' Billy said.

'Then winning the prize will be a very nice birthday present for you.' James Armitage put in. 'And, of course, for the school. Mister Skinter will give you a brand new exercise book, and your essay must fill around seven pages. You will not get the original back, so I think you should write out two copies in case one gets lost.' He glanced at the English teacher. 'Is there anything else, Mister Skinter?'

'Yes.' Horace Skinter said. 'The entry must be in spotless condition, with no blots, smudges, dirty finger marks, food or other *unmentionable* debris. For each of these sins, you will lose one mark. The writing must be your best, and two marks will be deducted for every spelling mistake, so don't make any. And no scribbled alterations. I cannot check your work as it is against the rules.'

'Yes, sir.'

Billy raced down the corridor and into the playground to find George and Sam. 'Well,' George said, 'what have you done to upset ole Skinter *this* time?'

Billy grinned from ear to ear. 'Nothing. He's put me in for the essay competition.'

'Blimey,' Sam said, as more of Billy's classmates gathered round to hear this amazing piece of news. 'Skinter's always *hated* you.'

'Yeah, but Billy's always top of the class for English,' another boy said.

Head Prefect, Maurice Andrews stepped forward. 'That's wizard, Billy,' he said. 'You deserve it.'

'No he doesn't.' All eyes turned to see Ginger Trueman pointing a finger at Billy. 'He aint been 'ere more than a few months. Why should he be picked?'

'Because,' Maurice Andrews said, 'he's the best in the class for English, that's why.'

Ginger Trueman pushed his face up against Billy's. 'I'm better 'n you,' he said, spraying Billy with spit, 'and I 'ope you don't win.'

Billy, who had so far kept quiet, gave the other boy a shove. 'Oh, go an' boil your head,' he said. 'That's if you can find a pot big enough to put it in.'

Ginger's fist came up and struck Billy on the chin. Billy hit back, Ginger took a tumble, and the other boys spread out to form a circle to watch the fight. Ginger scrambled to his feet, fists flew and he and Billy ended up on the ground, wrestling like two fighting dogs. When Billy felt Ginger pull at this hair, he yelled at the top of his voice. He tried to grab at the other boy's wrist but the illness over Christmas had left him weak and unable to defend himself. He lay there, very still. 'Just what I thought,' Ginger spat, unwinding his fingers from Billy's hair, 'you're a coward, Parkin. Can't even fight back.'

The Head Prefect stepping in and pulling the two boys apart saved Billy from further trouble. 'Quick, get up,' he said, 'Skinter's just coming out've the door.' He turned to Billy. 'He'll have your guts for garters if he sees you fighting again, Billy. And he'll stop you going in for that competition.' The others scattered as the two boys got to their feet, and Ginger stomped off, his face red with temper. Secretly, Billy hoped there wouldn't be any real trouble over this. He'd only just made friends with his old enemy, George, and didn't want to start a war with someone else.

That afternoon, he walked home from school with George and Sam. 'What are you going to write about?' George asked, as they sauntered along the road towards home.

'I don't know. I've done the Victorians but I s'pose I could do that again.'

'That'd be boring. All you'd be doin' is what you've already written before.'

'Mmm,' Billy said, and they all fell silent again.

'*I've* got a good idea.' Sam made the other two jump. 'Why don't you ask that man with the burnt face if you can write his story for the competition?'

'What man is that?' George asked.

'Oh, someone we went to tea with before Christmas You weren't there.'

Billy thought about Sam's idea. 'Would he let me, d'you think?' he said.

'Yeah, course he would. You'd have to go and ask him first though.'

The more Billy chewed it over, the more he was convinced that writing a story about a hero like Reggie Bassett-Wycliffe, or Skipper as he liked to be known, was a great idea. And it might even win Billy the prize.

Not only did Skipper agree, but also offered to let Billy use his study. 'You'll get a bit of peace and quiet in there,' he said, 'away from those sisters of yours.'

Each day after school, Billy spent every spare minute he could at Skipper's house, where Mrs Bassett-Wycliffe spoilt him with sandwiches of homemade plum jam, currant buns and glasses of ginger beer. Skipper repeated the story of his crash, but in more detail so that there was enough material to fill the seven pages required. Billy felt sorry when, at the end of the week, he'd finished making all the notes he needed to write his essay but cheered up again when Skipper offered his study once more. 'I don't go in there much, Billy,' he said. 'You may as well make use of it.'

On Saturday morning, Billy's mother handed him a small package. 'This is your birthday present,' she said. 'Your dad thought it would be a good idea to give it to you now instead of on the day, so that you could use it for the competition.'

Billy tore open the brown paper and pulled out a dark blue case. He opened it. 'It's a fountain pen!' he exclaimed. 'A Conway Stewart, just like the one Danny's got.'

'Yes. There was nothing to be found in the shops around here but dad managed to get this in a little shop down near the dockyard.'

'I've always wanted one of these,' Billy said. 'And I can write out my essay with it. Thanks, Mum.'

'Well, just take good care of it. If you lose it, you won't get another one.'

After a week of scribbling on an old notepad to put his notes in order, scratching out, changing this and that and checking Skipper's dictionary for spellings, Billy was ready to write it out properly in his brand new exercise book, with his new fountain pen. He made a second copy on some spare paper, which he gave it to Skipper to read.

'That's a good piece of work, Billy,' Skipper said, 'and Mrs B and I will keep our fingers crossed. No reason that I can see why you shouldn't win the prize.'

On the morning of his birthday, Billy was up early. Jess gave him a bottle of Stephenson's blue ink, and Shirley a bar of chocolate with one corner missing. 'I only ate *one* square,' she said, when Billy asked if the mice had been at it.

His mother was annoyed when he said he couldn't eat his breakfast. 'You shouldn't go to school on an empty stomach,' she said. 'Just have a piece of toast.'

Billy tried but the bread stuck in his throat and he pushed his plate away.

Everyone on the bus wished him good luck; everyone that was, except for Ginger Trueman who sat at the back with a face like a thundercloud. The others all ignored him.

'Take no notice, Billy,' Sam said. 'Before you came, Ginger was always top in English, but when ole Skinter put him up for the competition, he didn't win.'

'Well, *I* might not,' Billy said.

'Of *course* you will.'

The morning assembly seemed to Billy to go on forever. After the headmaster had addressed the children, droning on and on about nothing in particular, they said the Lord's Prayer and then sang the hymn "Onward Christian Soldiers." A short silence followed during which Billy thought he would fall over in a dead faint if they didn't get on with it.

'And now,' James Armitage said at last, 'for the moment we have all been waiting for - the announcement of the winner of this year's essay competition.' He turned to Horace Skinter who stepped forward, a sheaf of papers in his hand. 'Mister Skinter will read out the results.'

'I will read them in reverse order,' Horace Skinter said, the expression on his face giving nothing away. He fiddled around with his glasses, and then cleared his throat several times. The children began to get restless and a soft murmur of voices rippled across the hall. 'Silence!' he bellowed, having found his voice at last. The noise died down and he began reading out the results. 'In third place, Jane Hever of Hanover Road Girl's school, and in second, Donald Martin of Rollinson Street boy's.' He paused and all eyes turned to Billy. 'But it gives me great pleasure to announce that Billy Parkin, for his essay, "Skipper", is the winner.'

A loud cheer went up across the hall and Billy found himself hoisted into the air on the shoulders of some of his classmates and, in the tradition of the school, carried to the front of the assembly.

James Armitage and Horace Skinter shook his hand. 'Well done,' the headmaster said as the English teacher stood by with a broad smile on his face. 'Quite an achievement. And now, Mister Skinter will present you with your prize.'

Billy's eyes lit up when he saw the book, a leather-bound copy of Charles Dicken's "Oliver Twist". 'Thank you, sir,' he said.

'Well deserved, Parkin,' Horace Skinter said, giving him a pat on the back. 'Your name will be engraved on the school shield.'

Billy caught the bus home from school but instead of getting off where he usually did, he went on to the next stop. 'I want to tell Skipper,' he explained to Sam and George.

'I *knew* you'd do it, Billy,' Skipper said as he and Billy sat in front of a log fire munching their way through some of Mrs B's homemade scones. He stroked the good side of his face. 'What d'you want to do when you leave school, Billy?' he said, presently.

'Oh, I'll have to work where my dad finds me a job.'

'And what sort of job might that be do you think?'

Billy stared into the fire. 'Woodworking, I s'pect,' he said.

'And is that what you really want to do?'

'No, Skipper. I'd really like to work for a newspaper. Be a reporter or somethin' like that. *You* know - where I could write things.'

Skipper leaned over and patted Billy's knee. 'Well,' he said, 'if I were you, I'd talk to your dad about it. If you have to go out to work, you may as well do something you like. It won't be much fun, otherwise.' The old man stood up. 'But now, I think it's time you went home and told your mum the good news.'

Chapter Twenty-Seven

The Lost Cat

Billy flung open the kitchen door, threw his satchel on the floor and went into the living room where his mother was reading her Peg's Paper magazine.

'Guess what, Mum?' he said, waving his new book at her. 'I won the essay competition.'

She dropped her paper onto the floor. 'Oh, Billy, that's wonderful,' she said. 'Your dad *will* be pleased with you.'

'Yeah, an' ole Skin… Mister Skinter, shook hands with me an' said I'd done well.'

'Good heavens!'

'And my name's goin' to be put on the school shield.' He glanced around the sitting room. 'Where's Jess?' he asked, suddenly aware that his mother was on her own.

'She's gone out with Shirley. The cat has disappeared and they've gone to see if they can find it.'

'It's getting dark, Mum.'

'Yes, I know. Could you go and find them and tell them to come home, please?'

'But I wanted to go an' see Perizada.'

'Well, that'll have to wait. Besides, she's coming here tomorrow afternoon. I saw her in the village this morning and she told me about the wedding. She wants to sort out dresses for Jess and Shirley. You can tell her your news then.'

Billy sighed. 'Oh, all right.' He didn't want to go wandering around in the dark looking for Shirley. She would be bawling and making a fuss, and all because of a *cat*. 'But how do I know where to look? I didn't see Jess and Shirley when I came up the lane just now.'

'Go and try, anyway,' his mother insisted. 'Tell Shirley we'll all go looking tomorrow morning. And, Billy.'

'Yes, Mum?'

'Well done with the essay. You must go and tell Skipper. He'll be really pleased.'

'I've already seen him,' Billy said, 'on my way home from school.'

Billy, armed with a torch and a warning from his mother not to flash it around too much because of the blackout, set off to find his sisters. As he stepped out into the lane, he nearly jumped out of his skin with fright as he collided with someone. He peered through the half-light. 'Blimey, George, you nearly scared me to death,' he said. 'What're you doin?'

'Takin' Dougal for his walk,' George said. 'What about you?'

'Oh, my mum's sent me to find Jess and Shirley. Shirley's stupid cat, Raffles has gone missing and they're out here somewhere looking for it.'

'They won't find it in the dark,' George said, stating the obvious. 'I'll come with you if you like.'

'Yeah, thanks. Did you see anyone when you came up the lane?'

'No.'

'Well, we'd better go this way then,' Billy said. They set off towards the top end of Woodsmoke Lane, stopping every few seconds to see if they could hear anything. In a matter of minutes, the last of the twilight faded and they found themselves enveloped in darkness, with not a pinpoint of light to be seen anywhere. It felt eerie and sinister and Billy was glad of George's company. Billy jumped as something ran across his feet. He flicked his torch on.

'It's only a fox,' George said. 'Or a rabbit.'

'Oi, *you.*' A man's voice echoed down the lane. 'Stop waving that torch around in the air.' It was the local air raid warden, Tom Scully. 'You ought t'know better. There's a raid going on over Pompey and ...' Before he could finish his sentence, the wail of siren spread across the village. 'You'd best get home, just in case,' he went on. 'Now switch that blessed torch off.'

'My mum'll go mad when I tell her I can't find Jess and Shirley,' Billy said as he and George reached Billy's gate.

'Shall I come with you tomorrow morning?' George offered. 'To look for the cat, I mean.'

'If you like. The stupid thing's probably stuck up a tree somewhere.'

'What time?'

'About half-past eight.'

The two boys parted company and Billy went indoors. 'I couldn't find Jess and Shirley,' he said to his mother.

'It's all right, Billy, they're here. You must have missed each other.'

'Oh, *thanks*, Mum. Good job I didn't go any further than the top of the lane. I could've been out there all night.'

'Stop exaggerating and come and get your tea.'

'There's a raid goin' on over Pompey,' Billy said, as he tucked into his beans on toast and tried to ignore Shirley who was snivelling into her handkerchief and refusing to eat anything. 'An' the siren's gone off down the village, too.'

His mother poured tea for everyone. 'Yes, I know,' she said. Her forehead creased up in a worried frown. Billy knew that look, and what it meant.

'Will dad be all right?'

'Of course he will. Now, eat your tea up or it'll go cold.'

Shirley went on snivelling until Billy couldn't stand it any longer. 'Aw, shut up!' he shouted across the table. 'It's only a bloody cat.'

'*Billy*! That's enough of that.'

'Sorry, Mum but she's gettin' on my nerves.'

'That's no excuse for swearing and don't you ever let me hear you do it again.'

'*No*, Mum.'

'That was a pretty bad raid,' Billy's father said as he walked through the door at eight o'clock that evening. 'A bomb fell on the main road and the bus had to go all around town. The raids on

Portsmouth are getting worse again. Still, there's some good news. I've got the day off tomorrow.' He took the Evening News from his jacket pocket and spread it across the table. 'And there's talk of something big coming up to put an end to the war.'

'Let's hope so,' Doris Parkin said. 'Now then, Billy has something to tell you, Fred. Go on, Billy, tell your dad what you've done.'

Billy waved his new book at his father. 'I won the essay prize at school.'

His father's face lit up with a big smile. 'Well, fancy that.' He reached in his pocket and drew out a shilling piece. 'Well, done, Billy. Here's a little something to put in your money box.'

'Thanks, Dad.' Billy suddenly remembered Raffles. He didn't like the cat but neither did he want it to come to any harm. 'Tomorrow, could you help us find Shirley's cat, Dad? It's gone missing.'

'Of course I will, Billy. But now I need my dinner and a nap.'

Early next morning, Billy looked out of the window to see what the weather was doing. 'It's raining,' he said. 'We can't go.'

'We can't leave Raffles out there in this,' Shirley wailed. 'He'll die.'

'So what.'

'That'll do, Billy,' his father said. 'We've all got Wellingtons and Macs, so come on and get ready.' He collected a ladder from the shed, in case they found Raffles up a tree. 'Right,' he said, pointing to the bottom of the lane, 'you take the girls that way, Doris, and we'll go the other way. Then we'll meet up in the middle.'

George had turned up with Dougal, who was straining at his leash.

'Why did you bring Dougal?' Billy asked.

'B'cause he can smell cats, and barks at them,' George said.

The rain had now turned to sleet and hail which, gusting along on a strong wind, stung their faces and nearly blinded them. 'My eyes hurt, Dad,' Billy complained, 'an' I can't see where I'm going,'

'Then put your head down against the wind, and stop being such a nincompoop.'

They trudged on, through the mud calling out to Raffles as they went. 'I think he's dead,' Billy said presently, when he'd had enough of the wet and cold. 'We ought to go home.' His knees felt raw where the bottom of his Mac had rubbed against them, and water had seeped through the sole of one of his boots. Dougal hadn't barked once.

Fred Parkin stopped to get his breath. 'If we haven't found him by the time we meet up with your mother, well give up.' They set off again and a few minutes' later met her and the girls. 'Not a sign of him, Doris, and I think we've done all we can,' he said.

Shirley started to cry, and Billy put an arm around her shoulder. 'He'll come back,' he said. 'Cats often run off and stay away for days and days. You'll see.'

She shook herself free. 'What do you know about it,' she said. 'You don't even *like* cats.'

As the wet and weary searchers made for home, George let Dougal off his lead. The dog ran ahead and, when it reached Railway Cottage, stood at the gate and barked its head off. Billy ran on to see what all the fuss was about. To his astonishment, there on the verandah, in the dry, sat Raffles, licking his paws and cleaning himself. Billy felt sure the cat had a wide grin on its face. When Dougal bounded up the path, Raffles jumped to his feet, arched his back, and hissed and spat, and everyone laughed as Dougal turned tail and scampered back to George.

'I'd better get home,' George said. 'See you on Monday, Billy.'

'Yep. And thanks.'

'If that cat of yours goes missing again, don't ask *me* to look for him,' Billy said to Shirley, as he peeled off his wet things and rubbed himself dry with a towel. 'I always said cats are stupid and that one's even more stupid than all the rest of 'em.'

Chapter Twenty-Eight

Wedding Dresses

That afternoon, Billy opened the door to Perizada, who was struggling with what looked to him like a pile of velvet curtains. He let her in and she let them fall onto the table. 'They be heavier than I thought,' she said. 'I nearly dropped them in the mud.'

Billy eyed the pale green velvet. 'What're they for?' he asked, quite forgetting that a few minutes ago, he'd been bursting to tell her about his prize. Now, he had a horrible feeling that she was going to break her promise not to have him dress up in velvet as a pageboy.

'Your mum's going to cut them up to make wedding clothes,' Perizada said.

Billy looked at his mother. 'Well, you're not making any for *me,*' he said. 'I'm not dressing up in a velvet suit. Not for anyone.'

'Billy,' his mother said, 'Perizada wouldn't dream of asking you to do any such thing. And neither would I after what happened at the last wedding we went to when you told your little cousins that they looked proper little cissies, and made them cry.'

'I'm surprised at you, Billy,' Perizada said. 'But don't worry, these are going to be made into dresses for Jess and Shirley.'

'They're old curtains.'

'Yes, I know they are. But you can't buy material in the shops now, and when your mother makes them into dresses, no one will ever know.'

Billy thought it was a daft idea. 'I'm goin' to find my dad,' he said. 'He's making somethin' in the shed.' He made for the door and then remembered something. 'Oh, I nearly forgot, Perizada,' he said. 'I won the essay prize at school. I had a book, and my name put on a shield.'

Perizada smiled at him. 'I'm very glad to hear that, Billy,' she said. 'And *I* nearly forgot to wish you a happy birthday for yesterday.'

'Thanks.'

Billy pushed the door of the shed open and found his father leaning over the bench working on something that looked like a box. 'What're you making, Dad?' he asked.

'A tea caddy. It's a wedding present for your friend, Perizada.'

Billy stared at the delicate carving of flowers on the lid of the box his father held up. 'You didn't do that, did you, Dad?' he said.

'Yes, Billy, I did it when I was on fire watch in the dockyard. It was going to be for your mother, but when she told me about the wedding, we thought it would make a nice present.'

Billy ran a finger over the lid. 'I didn't know you could do things like that,' he said. 'It's good.'

His father straightened up. 'I used to be top of my class for woodwork at school,' he said, proudly. 'One-hundred percent I always got.'

'Blimey!'

'And I'll tell you something else, Billy. If I'd been allowed to do what I wanted when I left school, I'd have been a cabinet maker now, and we'd be rich.'

'Why didn't you?'

'My father said I had to leave school and pay my way, so I did, and took any job that paid well.'

Billy realised this was his opportunity to tell his father about his own wishes. 'Will I be allowed to do what I want when I leave school, Dad?'

'That depends on what it is you want to do.'

'I want to work for a newspaper, where I can write about things.'

'You mean you'd like to be a reporter?'

Billy crossed his fingers behind his back. 'Yes, Dad,' he said. 'I'd like to work at The Evening News in Pompey.'

His father smiled. 'We'll have to see. No promises, Billy but if it's possible, then a reporter you will be.' He turned back to his box. 'Now, I must get on but if you want to keep out of the way of the goings on indoors, you can stay here and watch. I'm just going to put a coat of varnish on the box to bring out the colour of the wood.'

Billy sat down on an old stool. '*Dad*,' he said, presently, 'is the war really going to be over soon?'

'I wish I could tell you, Billy. All I know is there are a lot of rumours going round, about some plans for a big campaign coming up to put an end to it. But I'm not allowed to talk about certain things I've been hearing at work.'

'When the war ends, will you still have to go to work every day?' Billy was looking forward to enjoying more of his father's company.

'I hope not. Why d'you ask?'

'Well, you're never here very much, *are* you?'

'It can't be helped, Billy. Most dads are away a lot, and just remember, some of them never come back home at all. Like your friend George's dad.' Fred Parkin finished his varnishing and wiped his hands in an old piece of cloth. 'Now I think you ought to go indoors and see what they're up to in there,' he said. 'And Billy ...'

'Yes, Dad.?'

'Not a word about the box to Perizada. It's to be a surprise.'

'All right.'

When Billy went indoors, he found his mother and Perizada drinking tea. The curtains, with bits of tissue paper pinned all over them, lay spread out over the floor. 'Look out where you're treading, Billy,' his mother said as he tried to pick his way over to his bedroom. 'We don't want your muddy footprints all over everything.'

'I want to go and see George,' he said. 'I've got some comics for him.'

'All right but don't be late for your tea.'

Billy was halfway down the lane when he saw George, with Dougal, coming towards him. 'I was just comin' to call for you,' George said, a big smile on his face.

'What're you grinnin' at?' Billy said, handing him the comics.

'He's gone.'

'Who?'

'My new dad. He's gone back to sea an' my mum says he won't be comin' back. Not *ever*.'

'He's not goin' to get drowned like your other dad, is he?'

George gave Billy a shove. 'Don't be daft,' he said. 'My mum had a big row with him and told him she didn't want him here any more.'

Billy hooked a big stone in the toe of his boot and kicked it up the lane. 'I bet you're glad. You didn't like him, did you?'

'No. He was always shoutin' at me and my mum.'

'Good job he's gone then.'

George let Dougal off the lead. 'Yeah.,' he said.

'I can't be out for long,' Billy said. 'My mum and Perizada are making stupid wedding dresses for Jess and Shirley out of old curtains, an' I've got to be back for tea.'

'Who's gettin' married?'

Billy clapped a hand over his mouth. 'I'm not supposed to tell anyone,' he said. 'I forgot.'

'Is it that witch?'

'I don't know. An' she's not a witch, either.'

George laughed. 'Yes you do,' he said. 'It *is*, isn't it?'

'Oh, all right. But you're not to tell anyone. She doesn't want the whole village to know.'

'I won't say a word,' George said, but Billy could tell by the look on his face that he couldn't wait to spread the news that the Mad Witch was getting married. The two boys followed Dougal into the woods, found a log and sat down.

'My dad says the war's going to end soon,' Billy said, presently.

'How does he know that?' George asked.

Billy tapped the side of his nose with one finger. 'It's secret,' he said, 'and he's not allowed to talk about it. But he says that something big is goin' to happen soon, and the Germans will give in.'

George thought about this for a moment. 'Will you be goin' back to Pompey?' he said. 'When it's finished I mean?'

'Yeah. I think we're going back in July anyway.'

'I'll miss you.'

Billy laughed. 'Fancy you sayin' that,' he said. 'What're you and your mum going to do?'

'She says we're goin' to live with my auntie Lilly in Bournemouth,' George said, 'but I don't want to go there. She's horrible. When we stay there, she makes me clean my boots *every* day, an' I'm not allowed to get down from the table until I've eaten everything on the plate. *And* I have to clean my teeth. *And* say thank you for the food before I've even eaten it.'

'You mean you have to say Grace. Well, it's better than havin' that rotten man for your dad,' Billy said.

'I suppose so.' George stood up and called to Dougal. 'I'd better be getting' back,' he said, 'else I'll get into trouble.'

They parted at the gate of Railway Cottage. 'See you tomorrow,' Billy said, '*if* you're allowed out.' He watched George amble down the lane, with Dougal running along behind, and was just about to go indoors when a boy on a red bicycle whizzed past him from the other direction. The boy stopped by Quirk's old home, threw his bicycle in the hedge and went through to where Danny lived.

Billy ran indoors. 'There's a telegram boy gone to Danny's house,' he shouted to his mother, who was still talking about weddings to Perizada.

His mother looked up, startled. 'It must be Tim,' she said. 'He's on active service somewhere in the Middle East.'

'Or it could be someone's birthday,' Perizada said, hopefully. 'Not all telegrams are bad news.'

'Shall I go an' find out?' Billy asked.

His mother shook her head. 'Certainly not, Billy,' she said. 'We'll find out soon enough.'

It didn't take very long for the news to spread across the village that Tim Palmer had been shot down in his aeroplane somewhere over Greece. For days after the telegram boy had called, people stood around in little groups talking about the tragedy.

'It's only a while since he was drawing those portraits at the fair,' said one old lady.

'Yes, and I heard he'd just got engaged to a nice girl from Yorkshire,' said another.

Harry Greentree, whose air force pilot son had been a close friend of Tim, spoke to Billy and his mother outside the chapel after they had attended a hastily arranged service for Tim. 'Another young life wasted,' he said, his eyes full of tears. 'And the Palmers can't even bring their son home to be buried here, where he was born.'

'Why can't they bring Tim home to be buried?' Billy asked.

'It wouldn't be possible,' Harry Greentree said. 'There are hundreds of men being killed out there, and where would they find the aeroplanes and ships to bring them all home?' He shook his head. 'And it's about time something was done to bring this damned war to an end.'

'My dad reckons there's something big coming up soon. Germany will surrender and that will be the end of it,' Billy said. 'Doesn't he, Mum?'

'Yes, Billy, he does.'

'I'll believe that when I see it,' Harry Greentree called over his shoulder as he walked slowly away downhill towards his cottage, muttering to himself.

Chapter Twenty-Nine

Long Trousers

'I'm taking Jess and Shirley to Portsmouth to buy them some new shoes for the wedding,' Billy's mother said, a week before the event. 'And it's Shirley's birthday on Monday so we'll be looking for a present for her while we're there.'

'I'll be six,' Shirley said, importantly.

'Yeah, I know,' Billy said. He was pleased that his mother hadn't insisted on him going with them. His father didn't have to go into the dockyard that day, and had asked Billy to help him clear out the shed. Billy had really wanted to go off for the day somewhere with George and Dougal, but helping his father would be better than trailing around the shops in Portsmouth looking for silly shoes.

The shed had a funny smell about it. Billy pegged his nose with his fingers. 'It didn't smell like this when the fox cub was here,' he said to his father, who had begun pulling boxes and old garden tools out into the garden.

'No, it smelled even worse,' his father said. 'Now stop moaning and give me a hand with this lot.'

They spent the next half an hour emptying the shed of old picture frames, boxes of books covered in mildew, toys, including a moth-eaten teddy bear, several dolls with china heads, and two tennis racquets full of holes. Billy pointed to a dolls house right at the back. 'I wonder who that belonged to?' he said, keeping his eye on two large spiders crawling up the wall close to where he was standing. Although he wouldn't admit it to *anyone,* he was terrified of spiders.

'The Foster sisters, I expect,' his father said. 'Help me to lift it up please, Billy, and we'll have a look at it.'

They carried it outside, set it down on the grass and Billy unhooked the clips that were holding the front in place. Apart from a carved wooden box in one of the bedrooms, the house was empty.

Billy lifted the box out and inspected it. 'It's like the tea caddy you made for Perizada,' he said. 'And there's a key in it. Could I open it, Dad?'

'Yes, but be careful.'

Billy turned the key, lifted the lid and took out four faded, sepia photographs. 'Look at these, Dad,' he said, passing them over. They were of two soldiers in uniform and their girlfriends, laughing into the camera and posing against a backdrop of the sea. 'I wonder who they are.'

'I think I can tell you that, Billy,' his father said. 'Look at the girls. They are wearing identical dresses and shoes, and they look exactly alike.'

Billy studied the pictures. 'The Foster sisters?'

'Yes. And the soldiers are, I think, from the Hampshire Regiment. Thousands of them died at the battle of Paschendael in France during the last war.'

'D'you think these two did?'

'I don't know, Billy, but it's possible. Maybe the sisters were engaged to them or something, and they, the soldiers, didn't come back. It happened all the time.'

'There's something else,' Billy said, diving into the box again. He pulled out a small bundle of letters tied together with a faded blue ribbon, and started to pull at the bow.

'No, Billy,' his father said, snatching them away from him, 'they're private. We mustn't read other people's letters.'

'Oh, go on, Dad.'

'No.'

'Can we read these then?' Billy held up some postcards embroidered in silk. 'They're from France.'

'No. Now put all this stuff back in the box where it belongs.'

But he was too late. Billy had already turned one of the cards over. 'It says,' he read aloud, "To my dearest Clarice. You are always in my thoughts. With all my love, Albert".

'I was right then. Those girls in the photos *are* the Foster sisters,' his father said. 'Now, Billy, please put everything back.'

'D'you think the soldiers did get killed, Dad?'

'Well, your mother didn't seem to think the Foster sisters were ever married, so I would guess that they both lost their boyfriends and never met anyone else.'

Billy put everything back in the box and closed the lid.

'I'll take that,' his father said, as Billy went to put it back inside the doll's house. 'I think it would be best if we kept it indoors.'

Billy shivered. He felt as if he'd uncovered a ghost. 'D'you think there will be another war after this one?' he asked presently.

'You're always asking me questions about the war, Billy, as if I know the answers. There've always been wars of one kind or another, but I hope we'll never see another one like the last, or this one.' His father fetched a broom. 'And now, I think we'd better get on with cleaning up before your mother comes back and wants to know what we've been doing all day.'

'What have you two been doing with yourselves while I've been out?' was the first thing she said when she arrived home with Jess and Shirley, later that afternoon.

Billy and his father looked at each other and burst out laughing. 'We've been working hard all day, Mum,' Billy said. 'Go and have a look at the shed.'

'I will in a minute, but first, here's a present for you, Billy,' she said, handing him a brown paper bag.

Billy tore it open and took out the contents. 'My first longs!' he exclaimed, holding the grey, flannel trousers up against him.

'Yes, and I just hope they fit you, Billy, because I can't take them back. I used the last of your clothing coupons to get them.'

'I'll try them on,' Billy said and disappeared into his bedroom, emerging a few minutes later wearing his new trousers. 'They're a bit long,' he said.

'You'll soon grow into them.'

'Are they for the wedding?'

'Well, yes. But it's time you went into long trousers and you can wear them to school afterwards.' His mother laughed. 'They will hide your skinny legs, Billy,' she said. 'I've never understood how it is that you eat like a horse but never put on any weight.'

Billy was annoyed with her for saying that. He couldn't help being skinny, and for some time he'd felt self conscious about his stick-like legs which were so thin that his socks were forever falling down around his ankles. All the same, none of the other boys in his class wore long trousers yet, and he would be the first.

'Look what I've got,' Shirley said, holding up a pair of black patent shoes with shiny silver buckles. And Jess has got a pair the same. And this is for my birthday.' She showed Billy and his father a box of handkerchiefs. 'They've got all the days of the week on them,' she said. 'There's one for every day.'

'Yes, I can see that,' Billy said, 'now can we go and look at the shed?' He and his father had only had a sandwich and a cup of tea all day and Billy needed his dinner. Besides that, he wanted to see George to tell him about his new long trousers.

Later, as he left Railway Cottage, he saw Danny coming down the side of Jethro Quirk's place, and called out to him. 'Wait a minute, Danny,' he said, 'I'll walk down the lane with you.'

Danny walked on as if he hadn't heard, and Billy ran to catch up with him. 'Don't you want me to?' he asked. 'I'm only goin' to see George to tell him about the new long trousers my mum's bought me.' Danny stopped and Billy could see that his eyes were full of tears. 'What're you cryin' for, Danny?' he said.

Danny took a handkerchief from his pocket, wiped his eyes and blew his nose. 'It's my mum,' he said. 'She's ill.'

'What sort of ill?'

'I don't know. She keeps crying, and she's got really thin because she won't eat.'

Billy remembered how he'd felt after Dave had been killed. 'Is it because of your brother, Tim?' he said.

'Yes. And our doctor says she's got to go into a rest home for a while to help her get better.'

'Oh. What'll you and your dad do while she's away?'

'My auntie Dorothy'll look after us I expect.' Danny began to walk on. 'I'm just going down to the village to see her now.' They walked on in silence.

'I'm sorry about Tim, Danny,' Billy said presently. 'I wish this war would hurry up and end.'

'So do I.'

They parted company at George's caravan, and Billy watched Danny until he turned the corner out of sight. It seemed strange to see Danny Palmer crying.

George was in the kitchen washing up when Billy arrived. 'What're you doin' that for,' Billy asked. 'That's a girl's job.'

'Well, I haven't got any sisters, have I?' George said, wiping his hands on a tea towel. 'Not unless you lend me one of yours.' They both laughed.

'You can have them both if you like,' Billy said. 'I'm fed up with all this wedding stuff. My mum's been makin' dresses for them, an' there's bits of velvet all over the place. I'm not allowed to move in case I tread on something.'

'Still, it'll all be over next Saturday,' George said. 'An' I don't mind doing the washing up. I get pocket money if I do it properly.'

Billy suddenly remembered why he'd come to see George. 'I've got my first pair of longs,' he said as he helped George clear up the kitchen. 'Grey flannels.'

'You lucky beggar,' George said. 'My mum says I've got to wait 'til I'm fourteen.'

'Well, I've only got mine because of the wedding, but she says I can wear them to school afterwards.'

'You're mum's nice.'

Billy thought about that. 'Yeah, I s'ppose she is,' he said. He rubbed his hand over his stomach. 'And she cooks lovely grub, too.

Chapter Thirty

The Wedding

The day before the wedding, Billy was in the Co-op getting the week's rations for his mother when suddenly, everyone stopped talking and turned to stare at a man who had walked into the shop. The stranger was tall, with lots of black, curly hair. He had a beard and wore a smart suit.

'Good morning, ladies,' he said, giving them all a wide smile. 'Lovely day, isn't it?' He joined the back of the queue behind Billy. 'In case you're all wondering who I am,' he boomed over the top of Billy's head, 'I'm Thomas Lee and I'm staying in a room at the Clipper and Bell until tomorrow when I'm getting married. I think you all know Perizada, my bride-to-be.'

A funny sort of silence descended over the shop. Then, 'Oh, we know *her* all right,' said Mrs Baggit who was, as usual, at the front of the queue.

'A very pleasant lady,' the woman behind the counter said. 'Comes in here quite a lot and is always most polite.' She threw Mrs Baggit a dark look. 'Which is more than can be said of some I could mention.'

Mrs Baggit looked daggers, 'Humph! That woman ruined my best hat,' she said.

The other customers looked at each other and sniggered. 'I daresay you asked for it,' said one. 'You ...'

Thomas Lee held up one hand. 'Now, now, ladies,' he said, giving them all another big smile. 'Let's not fall out. Perizada is who she is and I'm sure she wouldn't do harm to anyone, nor to anyone's best hat.' A ripple of laughter spread through the shop, and Mrs Baggit slapped her money on the counter, picked up her shopping and stormed out.

Billy liked the look of Thomas Lee. 'I'm Perizada's friend,' he piped up.

'Billy Parkin?'

'Yes.'

'I've heard all about you,' Thomas Lee said. The queue moved forward and Billy reached the front. 'I tell you what, Billy. I'm going your way to see Perizada, so you get your shopping and wait outside for me and we'll walk back together.'

'Perizada told me that you are an English teacher,' Billy said, as they strolled along the London Road towards home.

'That's right.'

'I like English, an' I want to work on a newspaper when I leave school.'

'That would be a good career,' Thomas Lee said. They turned into Woodsmoke Lane. 'And I believe you won an essay competition at school.'

'Yes, Mister Lee. I had a book for a prize, an' my name on a shield.'

'Well done. And I think you can call me Tommo.'

They stopped at Billy's gate. 'But you're a *teacher*,' he said.

Thomas Lee stroked his beard thoughtfully. 'Yes, Billy but I'm not *your* teacher, and I'd quite like you to call me Tommo. All my friends do.'

Billy didn't feel happy about calling a grown up by his Christian name but if that's what Thomas Lee wanted. 'All right, Tommo,' he said. 'I'd better go in now before the sun melts our butter ration. See you tomorrow.'

'Righto, Billy.' Tommo looked up at the sky. 'I hope it's as sunny tomorrow as this,' he said. 'Bye for now.'

Billy watched him walk to the top of the lane and disappear around the corner.

'Who was that man you were talking to?' his mother asked when Billy went indoors and dumped the bag of shopping on the table. 'I've told you before about not talking to strangers.'

'*Mum*, that's the man who's getting married to Perizada tomorrow.'

'Good heavens! He looks as if he needs a haircut and a shave.'

'Oh, *Mum*. He's a really nice man.'

'Well, if you say so, Billy. Now, let's get all this stuff put away. Did you get any eggs?'

'No. They didn't have any this week. And they'd sold out of dried egg.'

She gave a deep sigh. 'That means no cake for Sunday tea,' she said.

Billy woke early the next morning to the sun streaming through his window. He wasn't looking forward to sitting in a stuffy old chapel for the wedding but he'd heard there was to be a 'spread' afterwards, at the village hall. He could sit through anything for that.

'What's a 'spread?' he'd asked his mother last night.

'Just a few sandwiches and cake, I believe. And I think that Thomas Lee has managed to bring some sausages and bits and pieces from Cornwall.'

'Sausages! '

'Yes, Billy, and trust you to think about what you're going to eat. Do you never, ever think of anything but your stomach?'

'No, Mum,' he'd replied.

Perizada wore a flowery dress with a swirly skirt, and carried a posy of spring flowers. She'd done something to her hair. She had it all piled up on the top of her head, with just a few curly bits dangling over her ears. On a long chain, around her neck, a silver pendant in the shape of a crescent moon glittered in the sunlight. Billy thought she looked quite pretty. Jess and Shirley wore spring flowers in their hair, and the dresses his mother had made. 'You wouldn't know they were made from old curtains, would you, Mum?' he said, in a voice loud enough for everyone to hear.

'Why don't you get yourself a loudspeaker and broadcast it to the whole village,' she said. 'Now go on in the chapel and find a seat.'

The service seemed to Billy to go on forever. It looked as if the entire village had turned out to see Perizada marry her Tommo. The chapel was full of old people and the smell of mothballs and stale tobacco. Even Mrs Baggit turned up, in a red and white spotted dress, and a hat from which sprouted a bunch of tall, yellow and green feathers. Billy wondered if Perizada would get up to any of her tricks with it. He fidgeted around on the hard chair so much that in the end his mother lost her temper. 'For goodness sake, Billy, sit still,' she hissed in his ear. 'You're like a monkey on the end of a stick.'

'Can't I go and wait outside?' he asked.

'No, you cannot,' she said. 'And if I have any more of your nonsense, you'll get a clip round the ear, and nothing to eat.'

At last it was over and everyone went outside to see the bride and her new husband have their photographs taken. Billy's father, who'd had to go into work that day, had given Billy his Brownie camera with strict instructions on how to use it. 'I don't want to see feet or tops of heads cut off,' he'd said, 'so listen to what I'm telling you.'

'Yes, Dad.'

Despite the feelings of the villagers towards Perizada, many of them had contributed to the wedding feast, and Billy's eyes popped when he saw the spread laid out in the village hall. Plates piled high with sandwiches, jam tarts and fairy cakes, and on a large dish, steam rising from a mountain of sausages with dark brown, crispy skins. Skipper's wife had offered to cook them at home while the wedding was going on, so that they would be piping hot when everyone was ready to eat. She had also brought along some of her scones, and a pot of jam.

'Don't get excited, Billy,' his mother said when she saw him eyeing the two-tier wedding cake sitting in the middle of all the food. 'It's made of cardboard.'

Billy laughed. 'Don't be daft, Mum,' he said. 'How can a cake be made of cardboard? You're just pulling my leg.'

'Well, just you wait and see,' she said.

He went in search of Perizada who was standing with Tommo, just inside the door, shaking hands with guests who were still arriving. 'Is that cake really made of cardboard?' he asked, when he could get a word in. 'My mum says it is but I don't believe her. It looks real to me.'

'Sorry, Billy,' Perizada said, 'but your mum's right. Unless you have a good friend who keeps a shop, you can't get the stuff to make a real one.'

'Oh.' Billy was disappointed. He licked his lips, remembering the Christmas cakes his mother used to make before the war, with all that lovely marzipan and icing.

'If you wait a few minutes, you can take a picture of Tommo and me pretending to cut it,' Perizada said. She pointed to the tables where food was disappearing fast. 'But now you'd better go and get something to eat, otherwise there'll be nothing left.'

Billy didn't admit that he'd already had one plateful, and helped himself to some more sandwiches and a fairy cake. He almost dropped it all on the floor when his mother's voice in his ear made him jump. 'You can put all that back, Billy,' she said, 'and stop being greedy.'

'Aw, Mum.'

She fixed him with one of her stern looks and he put the sandwiches back. 'Could I just have this?' he said, holding up the fairy cake.

'No.'

'I'm goin' home,' he said, scuffing at the floor with the toe of his boot.

'Oh, no you are not. There's dancing in a minute.'

He laughed so loudly that everyone stopped what they were doing and looked at him. 'Dancin's for cissies,' he said, and his mother cuffed his ear.

Harry Greentree had brought along his gramophone and some records, and while Billy sat in a corner wishing he were somewhere else, the grown-ups danced to the latest songs. He felt fed up with being the only boy there. Perizada had invited George and his mother but they had already planned to go out for the day, Sam was in bed with measles, and Danny and his dad had to visit Danny's mother in the rest home where she had gone to recover from her illness. Billy swung his legs back and fore, scraping the toes of his shoes on the floor as he wondered if he could sneak out without being seen by his mother. He was just about to try his luck when

Harry Greentree suddenly cut short the music as, through the open windows, the wail of the air raid siren filled the hall. 'Stay right where you are, everyone,' he said, as he fetched his coat and tin helmet from a peg on the wall. 'I'll go and have a look to see what's what.'

'I don't know what all the fuss is about,' said Mrs Baggit, who had been keeping a wary eye on Perizada all afternoon. 'We never get any raids over here.'

Hardly had the words left her mouth when the heavy drone of what Billy recognised as a German bomber shook the hall to its foundations, rattling windows and doors, and sending cups dancing about in their saucers. He just managed to catch a bottle of vintage wine, given to drink a toast to Perizada and Tommo by the Clipper and Bell, as it toppled over and rolled towards the edge of the table.

The door flew open and Harry Greentree reappeared. 'Under the tables, quick!' he yelled. 'The swine's just unloaded a bomb.'

Everyone dropped to the floor and scrambled for shelter. 'A fat lot of good that'll do if the bomb falls on us,' someone said, and Billy thought of the air raid in which Dave and the other children had died. This time, it could be him and his mother and sisters. He wondered where they were. The last time he'd seen them they had been at the other end of the hall, dancing. He heard the whistle as the bomb passed overhead, then clapped his hands over his ears as, seconds later a massive explosion close by sent pictures flying off the walls, and shattered glass from broken windows scattering in every direction. For a few minutes, there was an eerie silence and then everyone crawled out from underneath the tables, brushed dust from their clothes and started talking all at once. Billy could hear Shirley screaming as his mother tried to calm her down. Dust and broken glass covered the tables, and the cardboard wedding cake had collapsed under the weight of a vase of flowers, blown off the windowsill by the blast. Perizada and Tommo stood at the end of the hall, staring in disbelief at the ruins of their wedding feast.

Harry Greentree blew the whistle he always kept on a string around his neck. 'Ladies, gentlemen and children,' he said, in a shaky voice, 'are any of you hurt?' A few of the guests had small cuts from the flying glass, but otherwise, no one had any serious injuries. 'That's a miracle,' he said as the all clear sounded.

'Where d'you think the bomb landed, mister Greentree?' Billy asked.

'No idea, Billy,' he said. 'But if you can all get together to sort out this mess, I'll nip down to the village and see what I can find out.'

'I saved this,' Billy said, handing him the bottle of wine.

Harry Greentree blew his whistle once more and held the bottle in the air. 'The landlord of the Clipper and Bell gave me this,' he said, 'to drink a toast to the happy couple, but I'm afraid most of the glasses are broken.' He handed the bottle to Perizada. 'But we'd all like to wish you and Tommo a long and happy marriage, and may all your troubles be little ones.'

Everyone laughed at the corny old joke, Perizada burst into tears, and Tommo, who looked as if he'd had a bag of flour thrown over him, said, 'We'd both like to thank you all for everything you've done. It's not that long ago that Perizada was telling me how the villagers didn't like her, but now,' he pointed a finger at Billy, 'thanks to young Billy Parkin here, that has all changed.'

Billy felt his face go bright red as everyone turned to look at him. Why did grown ups always say things that made you look silly? He managed to creep away from the others, who had now turned their attention back to Tommo, and went outside where he saw Harry Greentree talking to another man. 'That bomb fell in the field behind Woodsmoke Lane,' Harry Greentree said. 'No one hurt it seems, but a dirty great crater in the middle of Jeremiah Robson's crop of potatoes.'

Billy knew what that meant. Since coming to live in the village, he'd not been able to add anything to his collection of shrapnel bits. Early tomorrow morning, he'd get to that crater fast, to see what he could find.

Perizada and Tommo left shortly afterwards. They were spending their first night at her cottage before leaving, by train, for Cornwall the next day. Perizada put her arm around Billy's shoulder. 'I'll miss you, Billy Parkin,' she said. 'But I'll be back to sort things out at the cottage, before you go home to Portsmouth.'

Billy felt a lump come up in his throat. Now he'd have no one to run to when things went wrong. Still, it wouldn't be long before he'd be back in Pompey. July or August, he'd heard his mother say, which was only in a couple of months. He wandered back into the hall to help with the clearing up.

Chapter Thirty-One

Strangers in the Village

On a warm afternoon in the middle of May, when school had closed for the Whitsun holiday, Billy, George, Sam and Danny noticed some strange things going on in the village. They were off to search for tadpoles and as they walked in single file along the main road, clutching their empty jam jars, the ground began to vibrate. Billy looked up, expecting to see a German aeroplane but the sky was clear, and the air raid siren hadn't gone off.

'Thunder,' suggested George.

'Don't be daft,' Danny said. 'There's not a cloud in the sky.'

'Well, what is it then?' Sam said.

They all stopped walking and looked up and down the road. 'Look!' Billy shouted, pointing to a dark object coming towards them. 'I think it's an army tank.'

The vehicle lumbered towards them like a giant caterpillar, and as it passed by, the driver and two other soldiers in the turret waved at the boys. 'Where are you goin'?' Billy called out but the noise from a convoy of military vehicles following the tank, drowned out his voice.

'Crikey, there's hundreds of 'em,' he said to the others. 'Never mind about tadpoles, let's see what's goin' on.'

They turned back towards the village and jogged alongside a convoy of tanks, gun carriers, armoured cars, lorries, ambulances, and some strange looking objects which looked like flat-bottomed boats on wheels. As the convoy reached the village, it slowed down and everyone came running out of the houses and cottages to see what all the noise was. Billy ran up to the driver of the first tank. 'Where are you goin', mister?' he shouted.

'We aint goin' anywhere, son,' the big, black soldier said in a broad, American accent. 'We're staying right here for now.' He parked the tank at the side of the road and climbed down from his turret, followed by two other soldiers. 'What's your name?'

'Billy Parkin. An' you're a Yankee,' Billy said.

'I sure am. And my name's Sergeant Joe Lewsky, but you can call me Joe. And these two here are Elmer and Harvey. Joe took Billy's hand and shook it until Billy thought his arm would drop off. 'And are these all your pals?' He pointed at the other boys who were watching in amazement as the other vehicles pulled in and lined up behind the first, and dozens of soldiers spilled out onto the pavement.

'Yeah.'

'Do you kids ever get any sweets?' Joe asked, reaching into the pocket of his jacket.

'They're on ration,' Billy said.

Joe handed round some packets of chewing gum. 'Here y'are then. And if you come by tomorrow, I might be able to find you some chocolate. But for now, I gotta get my men set up so run along home and tell your mom that the army's here to stay.'

Billy's mother didn't believe him when he burst into the kitchen and told her the village was full of soldiers. 'What a load of old nonsense,' she said. 'What would soldiers be doing in a place like Horndean?'

Billy showed her the empty chewing gum packet. 'One of them gave me this,' he said, 'an' if I go back tomorrow, he'll give me some chocolate. He's a Yankee.'

'I want some chocolate,' Shirley piped up. 'Can I go with you?'

'Me too,' added Jess.

Their mother stopped peeling potatoes for a minute. 'You're not going anywhere,' she said, giving Billy an angry look. '*Any* of you. And as for you, Billy, you should have more sense than to take sweets from a stranger. That's of course, if what you say is true.'

Billy felt his temper rising. 'Why d'you think I always make things up?' he said. 'You wait 'til you go to work in the café on Monday mornin'. *You'll* see.'

'Well, your father will be home soon and we'll see what he's got to say about it.'

Billy's father arrived home two hours' later than usual. 'What a journey,' he said as he slumped in his chair and pulled off his boots. 'I've never seen anything like it in all my life. It looks like the army has taken over Pompey. Every main road is choc-a-bloc on both sides with soldiers, tanks, lorries and goodness know what else, from Southsea, up

Portsdown Hill and right along the London Road as far as the village. The bus could hardly get through in some places.'

Billy gave his mother a smug grin.

'And that's not all,' his father went on. 'You can't get into Pompey unless you live or work there. The police are stopping everyone, and if you haven't got your identity card, you're in for trouble with the law.'

'I met some soldiers, Dad,' Billy said. 'One of them, a Yankee called Joe Lewsky, gave me an' my friends some chewing gum an' he said he'd have some chocolate if we went back tomorrow.'

'I don't like Billy taking sweets from someone he doesn't know,' his mother put in quickly. '*Especially* a foreigner.'

Fred Parkin rolled himself a cigarette. 'They're all right, Doris,' he said. 'No one knows what they're doing here but something's in the wind, that's for sure.'

'Can I go back and see them tomorrow then?' Billy said, hopefully. He hadn't had any chocolate for ages, and not only that, he wanted to have a proper look around Joe's tank, if he would let him.

His mother frowned. 'Well, I suppose so,' she said. 'But if you take Jess and Shirley, you are not to let them out of your sight. Either that or you don't go.'

Billy rolled his eyes. '*Yes*, Mum,' he said.

The following morning, Billy was up early, hoping he'd be able to sneak out without his sisters, but they had beaten him to it and were finishing their breakfast when he appeared. His face fell, and Jess laughed. 'Mum thought you'd try something,' she said, 'so she called us while you were still asleep.'

'That's mean.'

'I was right though, wasn't I, Billy?'

Billy swung round to see his mother standing in the doorway. 'No, you weren't,' he lied. 'Anyway, nothin's goin' to happen but I'll watch them as best I can.'

'You never know with strangers,' she said, darkly.

Billy ate his breakfast as fast as he could and then he and the girls set off for the village. When they reached the main road, they stopped and stared in amazement. Since last night, more army trucks, tanks and gun carriers had arrived and set up camp on both sides of the road. Perched on top of their vehicles, the soldiers were having breakfast, tucking in to bacon sandwiches and tea. Billy looked around for Joe Lewsky.

'He was here yesterday,' he told the others. 'He's really tall, with a black face and three stripes on his sleeve.'

'Is that him?' Jess said, pointing down the road to where a line of soldiers, with their tin mugs, had formed a queue at a tea urn.

'Yeah, that's him.' Billy ran ahead to where Joe Lewsky was leaning against his tank, supping his tea, talking to Elmer and Harvey. He caught sight of Billy and the others and waved them over.

'Gee, you kids must've gotten out of bed early,' he said, with a big grin. He patted Shirley's head. 'And who's this cute little doll?'

'That's my sister, Shirley,' Billy said. 'An' where did you get those bacon sandwiches?'

Joe pointed along the road. 'That's our mobile canteen,' he said. 'An' the good folk of this little old town have kept us tanked up with water for our coffee ever since we came. And see that eating house over there? Well, they've promised us free coffee and fruit cake tomorrow, and as many apples as we can pick from their trees out back.'

'Our mum works in that café,' Billy said. 'An' this isn't a town. It's a village called Horndean.'

Joe lifted Shirley up in his arms and sat her on the tank. 'I'll remember that,' he said.

'Your skin is all black and shiny,' Shirley said, poking at Joe's face with a finger. He laughed. 'Sure is. And that's because where I come from, the sun always shines.'

'Where's that?' Billy asked.

'Florida. It's just about the sunniest place on earth.' He pulled a photograph from his jacket pocket and handed it to Billy. 'My wife and kids,' he said, proudly.

Billy studied it and then passed it around. In it, a large, jolly-looking black woman carrying a baby in her arms sat on the steps of a verandah. Squatting at her feet were three small children who looked like tiny versions of Joe Lewsky, and behind them in the background, a wooden bungalow.

'Is that your home?' Jess asked.

'Yep. It's not much to look at but I sure wish I could walk through that door right now.'

'Where are you goin'?' Billy said.

Joe shrugged. 'No idea, Billy,' he said. 'And I wouldn't be allowed to tell you if I knew.' He reached in to the inside pocket of his jacket. 'Now who'd like some candy?'

Three hands shot in the air and Joe pressed a bar of chocolate into each of them. 'Gee, kids,' he said, 'by the look on your faces, you 'd think I'd offered you a twenty dollar bill or something.'

'Thanks, Joe,' they chorused together.

'Sweets are on ration,' Jess said, 'and we can't get chocolate very often.'

Joe rolled his eyes, which made Shirley laugh. 'Jeepers, that's bad luck, kid.' He swilled down the last of his tea. 'Now, I've gotta get on with things so you all run along and have a look around and maybe come back tomorrow, eh?'

'Yeah. We will.'

'Will you have some more chocolate?' Shirley asked as Joe lifted her down off the tank. He ruffled her hair. 'For you, I think I might be able to find some,' he said.

'What are the soldiers doing in the village, Dad?' Billy asked later that evening. 'We talked to lots of them and they said they didn't know where they are going.'

'I don't suppose they do,' Fred Parkin said. 'But something big is in the wind, that's for sure.'

'D'you think they're goin' to fight the Germans somewhere?'

'That's more than likely.' And Billy had to be content with that.

The following afternoon, Billy's mother was late getting home from the café. 'I've been run off my feet,' she said. 'The place has been full of soldiers all day and the owner wants to keep it open 'til nine o'clock so I'm going back to help out. And if you and Jess want to earn some pocket money, you can come with me and do the washing up.'

'I'll do it,' Billy said, the thought of some money of his own overcoming his hatred of washing up.

'Me too,' Jess, who wanted one of the wooden pencil cases she'd seen in the village shop window, added.

Billy never forgot the next two weeks. He and Jess went straight to the café after school each day to help out, while Shirley wandered around making friends with the soldiers. On Saturdays, they were there for most of the day, serving, washing up and clearing away and, by the beginning of June, they knew almost every soldier by name. Billy was amazed at all the different places they came from. 'America, Canada, Australia,' he told his father, 'and even some from France and Poland. Sometimes, we can't understand what they're saying.'

'They're the Allied Forces,' his father said, and Billy noticed a strange, almost sad look pass across his face. 'And one day, Billy, I think we'll all have reason to be grateful to them.'

'Could we have some of them to tea?'

Fred Parkin shook his head. 'I think your mother's got enough to do, Billy,' he said. 'It'd be a lot of work.'

Billy turned to his mother. '*Please,*' he said. 'They've given us loads of chocolate and chewing gum. Oh, *go on,* Mum.'

She thought it over for a minute. 'I think I could manage a couple,' she said.

'Four?' Billy pleaded, thinking of Joe, his two buddies, Elmer and Harvey, and another soldier he'd made friends with called Andy MacDonald who came from Scotland.

'Well, all right as long as you give a helping hand,' she said.

'That sure am kind of your Ma,' Joe said, the next day when Billy asked if he, Elmer and Harvey would like to come to tea. Billy told them how to find Woodsmoke Lane and Railway Cottage, and then went to look for Andy.

Andy was sitting on one of the gun carriers cleaning his boots. Billy watched as the soldier smothered black polish into the toecaps and then spat on it and rubbed it in. 'Eeek,' Billy said. 'What're you doin' that for?'

'Makes them nice and shiny,' Andy said. He held one boot up to Billy's face. 'Look, you can see your face in it.'

True enough, Billy could clearly see his reflection in the toecap. 'Spittin's dirty, my mum says.'

'Oh, aye, it is. Now, what can I do for you, Billy?'

'D'you want to come to tea at my house tomorrow?'

Andy's freckled face lit up. 'Aye, that'd be nice,' he said. 'Just as long as you tell me how to find it.'

Billy repeated the directions he'd given Joe. 'See you at four o'clock then,' he said.

'Could I bring my mate, Duncan?'

Billy hesitated. His mother would probably go mad but he could hardly say no could he? 'Yeah, that'd be wizard,' he said. 'My mum won't mind.'

On the way home, he decided not to tell his mother about the extra visitor. Once this Duncan was there, she couldn't really say anything.

Joe, Elmer and Harvey arrived first, each carrying a cardboard box, which they dumped on the verandah. Billy's mother met them with a smile, which widened when Joe began opening one of the boxes. Inside there were tins of fruit, corned beef, condensed milk and dried egg. From the second box, Elmer produced some packets of tea and sugar, and the third revealed dried fruit and bars of chocolate.

'You really shouldn't have,' she protested but Joe held up one hand.

'It's our pleasure, ma'am,' he said. 'We've more than enough, and you folk are having a pretty rough time of it, so it's by way of saying "thank you" for making us feel so welcome.'

'Take it indoors and put it away in the cupboards, Billy,' she said, as if she was afraid of getting caught receiving what might be stolen goods. 'And you too, Jess.'

Billy, who was also wondering where all the stuff had come from, was glad that he and Jess managed to put it out of sight by the time Andy and Duncan appeared and that their mother didn't say anything about the extra guest.

'I'm sorry Billy's dad isn't here,' she said as they all sat down to tea in the garden. 'But he's had to work today. Something going on I believe.' She handed round a plate of Spam sandwiches. 'He works in the dockyard you know.'

'Yes, Ma'am, Billy told us,' Joe said.

'Is the war goin' to be over soon, Joe?' Billy asked as he helped himself to a slice of his mother's fruit cake.

'It sure is, Billy. Sooner than you think.'

'Tell us about yourself,' Billy's mother said. 'Whereabouts do you come from?'

'Sunny Florida, Ma'am, with my wife and four little kids. The best place on earth.'

'And you, Elmer?'

'My folk live in the Bronx in New York.' He gave Joe a funny look. 'Not quite as classy as Florida but it's home-sweet-home to me. I'm not married so that's where I hang out when I get the chance to go home.'

'Harvey?'

'It's good old Texas for me. My Ma and Pa have a ranch out there and that's where my wife, Kit and baby Harry are staying until I can get out of this goddam army, if you'll pardon the language, Ma'am.'

Billy noticed that while all this was going on, Andy's friend, Duncan kept chewing his nails and looking at his feet. He looked uncomfortable, as if he didn't really want to be here with the Americans. Billy turned to Andy. 'Whereabouts in Scotland d' you live?' he said.

'In a bonny wee place called Braemar in Aberdeenshire. My father's dead and I live with my Mam. I'm not married but there's a lassie waiting for me to name the day as soon as the war's over.'

'Your turn, Duncan,' Billy said.

Duncan went on looking at his feet. Then he stood up and, without a word, walked down the path to the gate and out into the lane.

Andy broke the awkward silence that followed. 'Sorry, everyone,' he said. 'You see, Duncan doesn't have a home. He lived in Coventry and all his folk died in an air raid there. Mother, father, grandmother, granddad, two sisters and an auntie. He could'na face telling you all about it.'

'Go after him, Billy,' his mother said, 'and bring him back.'

But when Billy ran out into the lane there was no sign at all of the soldier.

'Don't worry, Mrs Parkin,' Andy said. 'He'll be all right.'

Joe looked at his watch 'If you'll excuse us, Ma'am, we should be getting back. We've been told to stand by for orders and I don't think our Commander would be too pleased at finding some of his men were missing.'

'Thank you for coming,' Doris Parkin said. 'But before you go, Billy has something for you all.'

From his trouser pocket, Billy produced some bits of paper. 'These are our addresses for here and Pompey,' he said, handing one to each soldier. 'We want to hear how you get on when you leave here.'

'Sure thing,' Joe said, and the others nodded. 'And thanks for making us feel welcome.'

'It's been a pleasure,' Billy's mother said. 'And I'll see you in the café on Monday.'

The following afternoon, Billy's mother filled two brown carrier bags with fruit and handed them to him. 'Take these up for the soldiers,' she said. 'And see if you can find out how Duncan is.'

Billy struggled down the lane with the heavy bags and wondered how much longer the soldiers would be there, and where they would be going when they left. He'd miss them, especially Joe Lersky. Halfway along Catherton lane he stopped to rest his arms. It was then that he realised something was different. He could hear none of the noises the villagers had had to get used to over the past two weeks. The singing, shouting, banging about as they tinkered with their tanks and lorries. He dropped the carrier bags, ran to the corner and stared at the empty road.

They had gone, the only evidence that they'd ever been there, a few tank and tyre marks on the grass verges and some dustbins filled with rubbish. Trotting along on her horse, a girl Billy had never seen before called out to him.

'Good riddance to them,' she said. 'Now perhaps we can have our roads back at last.'

Billy scowled at her. 'Aw, shut up, *you* ' he said, and turned back towards home.

Chapter Thirty-Two

D Day

Billy stomped through the kitchen door and flung the bags of fruit on the floor. 'They've gone, Mum,' he said. 'All of them.' He put his head round the door of the living room. 'Where's Dad?'

'He didn't get home last night,' she said. 'He told me he might have to stay in the dockyard if the troops were on the move. Looks like the "something big" he was on about has started.'

'D'you think the soldiers will get killed?'

His mother gave a sigh. 'It depends where they're going, I suppose,' she said. 'But some of them will.'

'I hope Joe and the others will be all right.'

'Well, it's no use you worrying about it. There's nothing any of us can do, but I hope it means the end of the war isn't far away.' She handed him a letter. 'Here's something to cheer you up. A letter from Perizada, I think. It came yesterday but in all the fuss, I forgot to give it to you.'

Billy took it into his bedroom and tore open the envelope.

"Dear Billy,' he read

I hope you and your family are as well as we are down here in Cornwall. I do miss Horndean a little bit but Tommo and I are very happy. We are hoping to adopt a little boy

*whose mother can't look after him. He is only
one week old and we have asked her if we can
call him Billy. That's if we are accepted of
course. I think we have to wait a few weeks
before we can bring him home but I am so
looking forward to having him.*

*Will you let me know when you are going back
to Portsmouth because I want to come down
and see you before you go. I have some things
to do in the cottage, too.*

*Tommo has looked at this letter and corrected
all the spelling mistakes, but I am getting on
well with my English lessons.*

*Best wishes to your mother and father and the
girls, and I look forward to seeing you soon.*
Perizada"

Billy went back to the kitchen where his
mother was getting tea. 'Perizada wants to know to
know when we are going back to Pompey,' he said.
'She says she's coming down here to see us before
we go.'

'Quite soon I hope, Billy,' his mother said.
'We thought that you and the girls should finish out
the school term and then we'll be off.'

'Aw, Mum, do we have to go back?'

'Yes, of course we do. Now, what does
Perizada have to say'

'She and Tommo are goin' to adopt a baby and
call him Billy.'

Doris Parkin laughed. 'Well, all I hope is,' she said, 'that she doesn't have as much trouble with *her* Billy as I have with mine. Now let's have some tea.'

Billy's father didn't come home again that night. 'I doubt if anyone's allowed in or out of Portsmouth,' his mother said, the next morning. She handed Billy and Jess their milk money for school. 'It's going to be very funny at the café today. We're going to miss all those soldiers coming and going.'

At school on Tuesday, Horace Skinter stood in front of the class and rapped his blackboard pointer on his desk. 'Silence!' he bellowed, casting his eyes around the classroom, which brought the racket of thirty boys all talking at once to a halt. 'As you all know, the troops who have been stationed along our main roads for the past two weeks have gone. It seems that, late on Saturday evening, they moved on and we believe are heading for the coast. For what reason, we do not know. The headmaster will have his wireless switched on all day, and if there is any news, we will hear about it. Meanwhile, our lesson today will cover the construction of sentences. Now pay attention.'

But neither Billy nor most of the other boys could concentrate on what the English teacher was trying to teach them. Billy's mind kept wandering off in the direction of Joe Lersky and his family and the rest of the soldiers, and by the time class was dismissed for playtime, he'd not learnt anything at all about how to put a sentence together.

In the playground, groups of boys stood around talking about the about the events of the past twenty-four hours. Billy joined Sam and George. 'We had some of them to tea on Saturday,' he said.

'Yeah, so did we,' Sam said. 'How about you, George?'

George shook his head. 'No, we didn't. My mum had to go an' have her hair done or somethin'.'

Billy was just going to tell them about Joe and the others who'd come to tea when the voice of Ginger Trueman caught his attention. 'Who cares what happens to them anyway, Billy Parkin,' he shouted loud enough for everyone to hear. 'They was a nuisance, takin' up our roads an' pinchin' our water. My mum's glad to see the back of them. Not like your mum, asking them in for tea as if they was someone important.'

Billy swung round. Without thinking about the consequences, he clenched his fist into a ball and smacked the other boy on the nose. 'You shut your mouth, Trueman,' he yelled. 'They might all get killed.'

Trueman staggered back, clutching at his face as blood spurted from his nostrils. 'So what if they do?' he shouted back, then lunged at Billy and punched him in the eye. 'An' that's one I owe you, Parkin.'

Billy raised his fist again but Sam grabbed his arm. 'Pack it in, Billy,' he said. 'Old Skinters comin' over.'

'You'll be for it now,' George put in, remembering what happened when he and Billy had a fight.

Harold Skinter looked down his long nose at Trueman, who was still bleeding. 'What have you been up to?' he said. 'Looks like you've got a nose bleed.'

'He did it, sir,' Trueman said, pointing at Billy. 'I didn't do nothin'.'

Skinter raised his eyebrows. 'I didn't do *anything*,' he corrected.

'*Anything*, sir.'

Skinter looked from Billy to Trueman and back again. 'I have a feeling,' he said, 'that I overheard you, Trueman, making some disparaging remarks about the soldiers who spent some time in our village before going to war. Is that right?'

Trueman looked at his feet. 'I only said ...' he began.

'Did he or did he not?' Skinter asked Billy, who didn't know what the word "disparaging" meant.

'He said some nasty things, sir, and I hit him.'

After a pause during which Skinter's beady little eyes moved from one boy to the other, he said. 'Go and get your face washed, Trueman, And if I ever see you fighting on school grounds again, you'll get to feel the headmaster's cane.'

Trueman slunk off and Skinter turned to Billy, who was hoping *he* wouldn't be hauled off to the headmaster's office. The English teacher patted him on the shoulder. 'Well done, Parkin,' he said. 'Very well done indeed.'

'Blimey! Did you hear that?' Sam said, as Skinter walked away and George looked on with his mouth hanging open.

Billy laughed. 'Yeah. I guess he's not such a bad old geezer after all.'

'You sound just like one of them Yankee soldiers,' George said.

It was shortly after dinner break, in the middle of a Geography lesson, that the classroom door flew open and Miss Bennett, the Headmaster's secretary, burst in. 'They've landed!' she cried out at the top of her voice. 'On the beaches in Normandy.' She addressed the Geography teacher, Miss Harry. 'Mister Armitage says that when you have finished this lesson, you may send the boys home.'

A loud cheer went up from the class as Miss Bennett ran from the room to deliver the good news to the rest of the school.

Half an hour later, having found it no longer possible to hold the interest of her pupils, Miss Harry dismissed them.

Billy called in at the café on his way home. The place was empty and he found his mother leaning on the counter staring into space. She jumped when she saw Billy. 'What on earth are you doing here at this time of day?' she asked. 'Don't tell me you've come top in English again?'

He laughed, remembering the day he'd knocked tea all over the headmaster, and had run away from school. 'No, Mum. We've been let out early b'cause the troops have landed in France.'

'Yes, I heard it on the wireless here. I hope our soldier friends are all right.' She squinted at Billy's face. 'Have you been fighting again?' she said. 'You've got a black eye.'

'Well, there was this boy an' he said some rotten things about the soldiers, so I …'

'So you got into a fight with him?'

'Yes, Mum.'

She rolled her eyes at him. 'How many times do I have to tell you not to go around making trouble?'

'He asked for it. An' that's not all. Old Skint … *Mister* Skinter, who overheard what this boy said, told him off and said to me, "Well done, Parkin. Very well done indeed."'

'Good heavens! Well, I think I know why he took your side, Billy. Some time ago I was told by a lady in the Co-op that your mister Skinter lost his only son at Dunkirk, and not long after that, his wife packed her bags and went off to live with her sister. I doubt if he'd be very pleased to hear someone being nasty about the soldiers.'

'Poor ole Skinter. P'raps that's why he always looks so miserable.' Billy looked around the empty cafe. 'It seems funny in here without the soldiers, doesn't it, Mum? Sort of *ghostly*.'

'Yes. They were good fun.' She looked up at the clock on the wall. 'Shirley'll be here in a minute, and I expect your dad will come home tonight so run along home and peel some potatoes for dinner. I won't be long.'

After they'd eaten, Billy's father switched on the wireless and turned up the sound as news came in about the Normandy landings. The newsreader droned on about the Allied Troops, who were making progress but had suffered heavy losses.

'What does that mean, Dad?' Billy asked.

'It means that many of the soldiers have been killed, Billy. They don't know the number yet but …'

Billy didn't wait to hear any more. He ran from the cottage, across the back garden and into the copse beyond. There he sat on a log and thought about Joe Lersky and the others. He wished they'd never come to the village and that he'd never got to know them.

'What're you doin', Billy?' Billy nearly jumped out of his skin as Meg's face appeared over the top of a tangle of bushes.

'You frightened me to death, you did,' he said. 'An' I'm just thinkin' about things, that's all.'

'What things?'

He wished she'd go away and leave him alone. 'The soldiers,' he said. 'My dad's been listening to the news, and lots of them have been killed.'

She inched her way through the bushes and sat down beside him. 'I know,' she said. 'My mum and dad are listening too.'

'Did you make friends with any of them?' Billy asked.

'No. My mum doesn't like me talking to strangers and she wouldn't let me go up there.'

'Oh. Well, you could've come with me, Jess and Shirley,' Billy said. 'An' they were all right. They didn't do anything bad.'

'When are you going back to Portsmouth?' Meg asked, changing the subject.

Billy picked up a twig and threw it into the air. 'Soon,' he said. 'When school's finished I think.'

She took hold of his hand. 'I'll miss you, Billy,' she said. 'I quite like you really.'

Billy smiled at her. He thought she looked pretty with the sun on her auburn hair. 'You look as if your head is on fire,' he said.

They both laughed and she leaned over and gave him a quick peck on the cheek. 'I'll come and visit you,' she said, 'and we can go to the pictures together if you like.'

Billy thought this over. He didn't really like girls but Meg wasn't too bad. 'Yeah, all right,' he said. 'That'd be wizard.'

They both stood up. 'Cheer up, Billy,' Meg said. 'Your soldier friends will be all right. I *know* they will.'

Chapter Thirty-Three

Going Home

'What are Doodlebugs, Dad?' Billy asked one Sunday morning when he was helping his father clear up the garden, ready to hand back Railway Cottage to the Foster sisters. The date for moving back to Portsmouth had been settled, and they would be leaving Woodsmoke Lane on the twenty-second of July.

'They're some kind of new weapon the Germans have been firing over here. Why d'you ask?'

'Some boys in my class said they're aeroplanes that fly without a pilot. That's daft, isn't it?'

Fred Parkin shook his head. 'Daft it may sound, Billy but it's true. They're called Flying Bombs, and the Germans are firing them over the English Channel from somewhere in France. We haven't had any over Portsmouth yet but we'll know all about it when we do.' He stopped to roll a cigarette. 'I've heard that they make a horrible droning noise and when the fuel runs out, the engine stops and there's about fifteen seconds before they hit the ground and explode.'

'Blimey. That's horrible.'

'Yes, and if ever you hear one, you should get down on the ground where you are and not try to run for shelter.'

'Well, I hope we don't get any over here,' Billy said.

'I shouldn't think so. They only carry so much fuel and I doubt if they'd make it as far as Horndean.'

Not wanting to hear any more about pilotless aeroplanes, Billy changed the subject to something more cheerful. 'Perizada's coming to see us next week,' he said, 'an' Mum says she can come to tea. An' the week after, I'm having a party up in the woods with all my friends.'

Billy's father puffed on his cigarette. 'That'll be nice for you, Billy, and then it's back to Pompey and the end of the war I hope.'

Billy pulled a face. 'I wish we didn't have to leave here,' he said. He sniffed the air. Even though it was the middle of summer, some people still had to light fires to heat up their water, and the smell of wood smoke filled the garden. 'I love the smell of burning wood,' he said.

Perizada's visit was a short one. She arrived on the following Friday, came to tea on Saturday and went home on Monday. Billy was amazed to see the change in her. Gone was the long hair hanging over her shoulders like a pair of curtains; she'd had it cut short, which made her look younger. She no longer wore gold hoops in her ears or jangly bracelets and, instead of her usual, brightly coloured long dress, she had on a grey two-piece costume, shoes with high heels, and she carried a handbag.

'Blimey!' he said when he first saw her. 'You look different.'

'I'm a school teacher's wife now, Billy,' she said. 'And have to look respectable.' She gave him one of her wicked smiles. 'But once Tommo and I have settled down for the evening and can be sure none of the old busybodies from the village will come calling, I change back into my old things.'

'D'you like living in Cornwall?'

'Oh, yes. Although I do miss Horndean a little bit. But once the baby comes to us, I won't have time to worry about anything else.'

'When will you be able to take him home?' Billy's mother asked.

'In about three weeks, I hope. As long as his mother doesn't change her mind before we sign all the papers.'

After tea, Perizada opened her handbag, took out two small items wrapped in tissue paper and handed one each to Jess and Shirley.

'What is it?' Jess asked, holding out the tiny, silver figure, crouched on a mushroom, for her mother to see.

'It's a Joan the Wad good luck charm from Polperro,' Perizada said. 'Known as the Queen of all the lucky Piskies, the story goes that, if you always carry it with you, it'll bring you good luck. Sometimes it will play mischievous tricks on people but only in fun.'

'Mine looks like an Elf,' Shirley said. 'Is it magic?'

'Well, in a way it has magic powers,' Perizada said. 'But not *real* magic, like Wizards and Witches can do. Just keep it in your pocket and it will bring you good luck.' She delved once more into her bag, brought out another object and handed it to Billy. 'And this is for you.'

He opened the tissue paper and lifted out the brass figure of a wizened little old man.

'It's a Jack 'o' Lantern key ring,' Perizada said, 'King of the Cornish Piskies. Just like Joan the Wad, he will bring you good fortune but may also play pranks on you, so be warned.'

Billy laughed aloud as if he didn't believe a word of it, and his mother gave him a dark look. 'Thanks, Perizada,' he said. 'I'll take it with me wherever I go.'

The following Saturday, Billy was up at dawn to get ready for the party. His mother was in the kitchen making Spam sandwiches. 'Oh, not Spam again, Mum?' he complained. 'Couldn't I have cheese?'

'No, you cannot,' she said. 'And if you are going to moan, you'll not get anything at all.' She handed him a paper bag. 'Go and pick some plums to take with you. And make sure there's enough for Jess and Shirley.'

He went out into the orchard, muttering to himself about having to take both his sisters along. He didn't mind Jess so much, but Shirley would spoil the fun for everyone.

They set off into the woods with their sandwiches, fruit and a bottle of Tizer their mother had managed to get in the Co-op. The others were already there when they arrived. George, Danny, Sam, Nancy, Meg and one or two other boys from Billy's class who had been invited.

'Let's play Tarzan games first,' Danny said. 'Get in line and we'll take turns.'

'Shirley can't do it,' Billy said. 'She's too small.'

Shirley began to scream and stamp her feet. 'Here,' Meg said, handing her a skipping rope. 'I brought this for her.'

With peace restored, the others began their game of swinging from tree to tree, the boys yelling at the tops of their voices "Aaah-eee-aaah-eeee'. The girls, who were told they couldn't do that because they were Jane and not Tarzan, stood around watching.

They were all making so much noise that Billy could never quite remember when it was that he heard the monotonous drone of what he thought was an aeroplane. The wail of the air raid siren put an end to their game, and they all stood still and listened.

Clunkety clunk, clunkety clunk. Billy knew, from what his dad had told him, what it was. 'Get down everyone,' he shouted, pushing Shirley onto her face and pinning her to the ground with one arm. 'It's a Doodlebug.'

They all flung themselves to the ground and waited. The clunkety clunk stopped and the fear that had gripped Billy when he and Jess were machine-gunned, gripped him again. He lay quite still and whispered to Shirley not to move. Everything went quiet and Billy's stomach turned over. He heard a swishing noise, like the wind blowing through the trees, and then an explosion shook the ground. No one moved for several minutes until a white-faced Jess stood up, brushed the woodland debris from her clothes and said she was going home.

'Wait 'til we've had our picnic,' Meg said. 'It's all over now anyway. The all clear's just going off.'

Jess hesitated. 'All right,' she said. 'But if the siren goes again, I'm off.'

They ate their picnic, but the arrival of the Doodlebug had spoilt the party and, after a few games of Hide and Seek, and Chase they decided to pack up.

'Before you go,' Danny said, 'We want to give you something to remember us by.' He took a parcel from his food bag and handed it to Billy. 'It's for all of you,' he said.

Billy tore open the brown paper and pulled out a dog-eared book entitled "Horndean through the Ages."

'There's lots of pictures for Shirley to look at, 'Danny went on. 'That is until she's old enough to read it.'

'Thanks, Danny, and all of you,' Billy said. 'I'm goin' to miss Horndean.'

'And me,' Jess put in. 'It's been lovely living here.'

'How about you, Shirley?' Danny asked.

'I want to go back to Portsmouth,' she said. 'I don't like it here.'

'I wonder where that Doodlebug landed,' Billy said as he, Jess, Shirley and Meg strolled back to up the lane.

Jess pointed to what looked like smoke coming from somewhere behind Perizada's cottage. 'Over there,' she said. 'Look.'

They ran to the top of Woodsmoke Lane. 'It's all right,' Billy said. 'It's in that field where Bruno the bull used to be. It only *just* missed Perizada's cottage though.'

They climbed onto a five-barred gate to have a better look at the remains of the Doodlebug. 'Not much to see 'cept a hole in the ground,' Billy said, disappointingly.

On Saturday the twenty-second of July, Billy and his family waved goodbye to Railway Cottage and Woodsmoke Lane. He felt choked up as they reached the bottom, and turned for one last look. 'When I'm grown up,' he said to his mother, as they moved on, 'I'm goin' to buy a house and live here.'

She smiled. 'I'm not sure that you'll ever be grown-up, Billy,' she said.

It took Billy a long time to settle back into his home in Portsmouth. He went back to his old school where he found so many new faces that he hardly knew anyone at all. 'I don't know where all the others have gone,' he said to his mother. 'There's a boy called Jack who sits next to me in class. He came to live here with his grandmother because his mum's ill. I quite like him.'

'Well, maybe the others have been evacuated,' his mother said. 'Don't forget there have been lots of air raids these past few months.'

'Could I ask Jack to tea?'

'Yes, of course you can, Billy. I expect he'd like that.'

'And, Mum?'

'Yes?'

'We haven't heard from the soldiers yet, have we? D'you think they've been killed?'

His mother reached into her apron pocket and drew out a letter. 'It's funny you should ask that, Billy,' she said. 'This came yesterday. It's from Harvey.' She gave the letter to Billy to read.

"Dear Mrs Parkin,

I hope that you, your husband and the children are keeping well. I am sending this to Portsmouth as I think you may be back home by now.

At the moment I am in a field hospital (can't say where). I caught the tail end of some gunfire but not too badly hurt. I'm sorry to have to tell you that Joe and Elmer weren't so lucky. They both died of their injuries. Poor Billy will be upset, as he and Joe were good friends for the short time we stayed at Horndean.

As for Andrew and Duncan, I'm afraid we got separated and so I don't know what became of them. If I hear of anything, I will let you know.
With best wishes to you all,
Harvey"

Billy handed the letter back without a word.

He and Jack Finlay became firm friends. Jack was small for his age, with sandy coloured hair and a face full of freckles. Billy liked him because he laughed a lot. They went to the Saturday morning pictures at the Regal together, played football in the park, and even swapped stamps the way he and Dave used to. He often came to tea with Billy but never asked Billy to his grandmother's house. 'She's old,' Jack said, one day when Billy asked him why. 'She doesn't like boys.'

After a while, Billy stopped thinking much about Railway Cottage and Woodsmoke Lane. He was looking forward to his fourteenth birthday in January when he would be old enough to leave school and, if lucky, find a job at the Portsmouth Evening News. He never went anywhere these days without his Jack O Lantern to bring him good luck.

Billy's father always brought the Evening News home with him and, one evening just before Christmas, he spread it out on the table and jabbed a finger at a picture on the front page. 'Come and have a look at this, everybody,' he said. Billy, his mother, Jess and Shirley crowded round, all trying at once to see what he was pointing at.

'It says it's Railway Cottage,' Billy cried. 'It's been burnt down.'

His mother peered at the picture of the charred skeleton that was all that was left of the cottage. 'What a terrible thing to happen,' she said, and Billy saw her eyes fill with tears.

'It would have been worse if we'd been in it,' his father said.

After that, Billy began to settle down. He would never forget Railway Cottage, the smell of Woodsmoke, and some of the friends he'd made there. He was still in touch with Perizada, and Meg had promised to come and stay.

'I've got lots of things to look forward to,' he told his mother. 'And the war'll soon be over, won't it?'

'Yes, Billy. It will.'

The End

June 1945

Billy sat at his desk chewing the end of his pencil. He was in his last term at school and couldn't wait for the day to come when he'd walk out of the gate for the last time.

The war in Europe had ended on May the eighth. Since then there had been street parties, school parties, family parties, parties in the Guildhall Square; in fact he couldn't think of any place where, for the past few weeks, there hadn't been a party of some sort or another going on and he was bored with them. All he wanted was to start his first job at the Portsmouth Evening News, where he'd had an interview and been accepted as a Messenger Boy.

He gazed out of the window and fell to thinking about Horndean. Since the fire, which had destroyed Railway Cottage, he'd not thought much about it, but a letter from George this morning, brought back memories. Poor George was moving with his mother to Bournemouth to live with his Auntie. Billy knew that George didn't want to go there where he'd be bullied and picked on by the old lady.

'I'll run away,' he said in one part of his badly written letter. 'Yes, that's what I'll do.' Billy smiled to himself at the thought of George Bunn having the courage to do something as daring as that.

Billy tried to conjure up a picture of Perizada but she'd changed so much the last time he'd seen her that he couldn't. She still wrote to him and said that when he'd been at work for awhile and had saved some money, he could come down to Cornwall for a holiday with her, Tommo and baby Billy. "I love being a mother," she'd written, "and we hope soon to adopt a sister for Billy." Billy wasn't sure if he wanted to go all the way to Cornwall just to see babies.

Danny sent postcards now and then but he was busy studying hard so that he could get into a university later on. He said that Sam and Nancy were still living in The Avenue but that he didn't see them much. He didn't mention his mother at all.

As for Meg, well she had promised to visit Billy in Portsmouth, and she had already kept that promise twice. He felt happy when he thought about Meg. The last time she'd come down, he'd taken her to the Regal and spent all his sweet coupons on some chocolate for her. He liked her and hoped she'd be able to stay longer in the school holidays. He could always catch a bus and go to Horndean to see her but his mother thought it unwise to go back and see the ruins of Railway Cottage. 'It'll only make you miserable, Billy,' she'd said when he'd suggested it. 'Best to remember it as it was when we left it.'

The ringing of the bell for home time brought Billy back to the present with a start, and the banging of desk lids and the scraping of chairs on the wooden floor signalled the end of another boring day. He and Jack left the school together and, as they went through the gate, Billy stopped for a moment, as he always did, to stare across the road at the space where Dave's house once stood.

'My best friend was killed over there,' he said.

'Yeah, I know,' Jack replied. 'You told me before.'

They parted company at the corner, and Billy walked on.

'Wait for me, Billy.' It was Jess, running to catch up with him. She stopped and clutched at her side.

'What's the matter with you?' he said.

'Stitch,' she panted, her face screwed up with pain.

'Serves you right for runnin' after me.'

She laughed and took a swing at him with her satchel.

Billy caught it by its strap. 'The last time you did that,' he said, 'we got machine-gunned in the street.'

'And then moved to Horndean,' she said.

'Yeah.'

'D'you wish we were still there, Billy?'

Billy stood still and looked across the road to the Regal cinema, and the fish and chip shop next door to it where, for a halfpenny you could still get a bag of greasy scraps. He thought about the seafront, which was just five minutes' walk from where they lived. And there was the football pitch just up the road.

'Nah,' he said, presently. 'I liked it at Horndean but it's nice to be back in Pompey.'

Glossary of Terms

Anderson:- A WW2 air raid shelter made of curved steel and set about four feet into the ground.

Chad:- A cartoon character popular during WW2, usually pictured sitting on a wall. The caption always started with "what no …"

Ack Ack guns:- Anti-Aircraft guns.

Cordite:-An explosive material containing cellulose nitrate, sometimes used in bombs.

Pompey:--A slang name for Portsmouth

Stuka:- A one-engined, two-seater German dive bomber aeroplane

Shrapnel:- Fragments from an exploding bomb or shell.

W.V.S:- Acronym for the Women's Voluntary Service whose members were noted for their good works during WW2.

Printed in the United Kingdom by
Lightning Source UK Ltd., Milton Keynes
138382UK00001BA/238/P